喚醒你的英文語感！

Get a Feel for English !

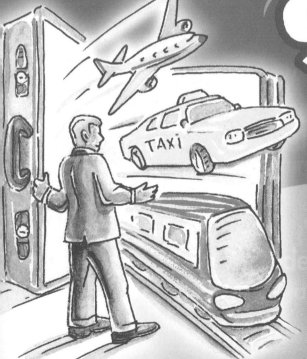
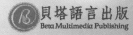

Preface

Why are you looking at this book? Odds are you're a business person who has to travel as part of your job. Maybe it's your first time; or maybe you've spent so much time on the road you feel totally at home living out of a suitcase in hotel rooms. Either way, if you do business in the global village, travel is often a necessity. Are you up for the challenge?

Having the right vocabulary to interact with English speakers can help to put your mind at ease before you go, and learning the right things to say can be a huge asset when it comes to smoothing out problems you're bound to run into. The bottom line: English can help you get what you want when traveling and doing business.

Beta's *Overheard on a Business Trip* gives you the tools you need to get your job done. Use this book and the CDs to prepare before your next trip. And don't forget to take it with you—this handy, lightweight volume makes the perfect traveling companion.

Imagine the utility of having an easily referenced pocketbook at your fingertips to help with every aspect of your trip, from beginning to end.

From setting up meetings to getting around the airport; from staying in hotels to sightseeing; from making sales pitches to negotiating contracts; from giving speeches to making toasts. No matter what the situation, Beta's *Overheard on a Business Trip* has you covered!

Have a nice flight.

Jason Grenier

作者序

　　你為什麼看這本書？很可能你是生意人，而且在工作時必須出差。也許你是第一次出差；也許你已經花了不少時間在外奔波，而且對於靠一只皮箱在飯店的房間裡過日子覺得十分自在。無論是哪一種，只要你在地球村裡做生意，出差往往就是免不了的事。你準備好接受挑戰了嗎？

　　能以適當的字彙和英語系人士往來可以使你在出發前放鬆心情；而學會要說什麼才恰當也大有助於緩和你勢必會碰到的問題。總而言之，英語能幫助你在出差和做生意時達到你的目的。

　　貝塔出版的《出差 900 句典》給了你所需要的方法來把事情做好。利用本書及所附的 CD 來為下次的旅程作好準備，而且別忘了把它帶在身上，這本輕薄短小的書可說是旅行的最佳良伴。不妨想想，隨身攜帶一本方便查閱的口袋書，以便應付行程中從頭至尾出現的各種狀況，這會有多方便？

　　從安排會面到在機場行動，從待在旅館到觀光，從推銷生意到協商合約，從發表演說到敬酒，無論是哪種情況，貝塔出版的《出

差 900 句典》皆可幫你搞定！

　　祝你旅途愉快。

Jason Grenier

出差進行曲 (by Brian Greene) CD1 02

出差 900 句典　出差 900 句典　出差 900 句典
Take this book with you on your business trip
Business trip

出差 900 句典　出差 900 句典　出差 900 句典
Take this book with you on your business trip
Business trip

Seize the day, make your play, extend your stay
Nothing's going to get in your way
Pave the way for a raise on your business trip
Business trip
Business trip
Business trip

出差 900 句典　出差 900 句典　出差 900 句典
Take this book with you on your business trip
Business trip

出差 900 句典　出差 900 句典　出差 900 句典
Take this book with you on your business trip
Business trip

出差 900 句典　　出差 900 句典　　出差 900 句典
帶著這本書去出差
出差

出差 900 句典　　出差 900 句典　　出差 900 句典
帶著這本書去出差
出差

把握當下，執行計畫，多停留點時間
沒有什麼事會與你作對
在出差之路上為加薪鋪路
出差
出差
出差

出差 900 句典　　出差 900 句典　　出差 900 句典
帶著這本書去出差
出差

出差 900 句典　　出差 900 句典　　出差 900 句典
帶著這本書去出差
出差

單元說明與使用方法

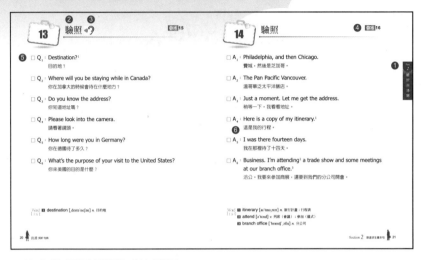

❶ 依本書分類架構做成的側標。

❷ 用語的主題。

❸ 標示此圖 ♫?，表示此部分為出差時可能聽到的話；未標示者，則為讀者說的話。

❹ CD 軌數。

❺ 將你習慣使用的用語，在 □ 中打勾，下次你可更快找到它的位置。

❻ 某些頁面為相對應的問答，以 Q 標示問句，以 A 標示其答句。

查詢小撇步：先由 ❶ 側標找到所需用語的分類，再由 ❷ 去搜尋用語的主題，很快就可以找到你所需要的句子。

Contents

作者序 ……………… *iii*

出差進行曲 ……………… *vii*

單元說明與使用方法 ……………… *ix*

1
Section 行前準備基本句

01 探詢拜會的可能 ……………… *02*

02 接受／確認邀請 ……………… *03*

03 蒐集商展訊息 ……………… *04*

04 登記參加商展 ……………… *05*

05 預訂飯店 ……………… *06*

06 打聽會展的最新消息 ……………… *07*

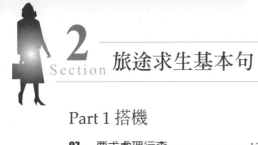

2
Section 旅途求生基本句

Part 1 搭機

07 要求處理行李 ················ *12*
08 要求換位子 ················ *13*
09 要求升等 ················ *14*
10 要求協助填寫出入境表格 ················ *15*
11 要求服務 ················ *16*
12 要求轉機 ················ *17*

Part 2 驗照與通關

13 驗照 ■♪ ················ *20*
14 驗照 ················ *21*
15 申報繳稅物品與檢疫 ■♪ ················ *22*
16 申報繳稅物品與檢疫 ················ *23*
17 違反規定 ■♪ ················ *24*

18　違反規定 ·················· *25*

19　遇上大麻煩 ⑴ ·················· *26*

20　遇上大麻煩 ·················· *27*

Part 3 在機場

21　換錢 ·················· *30*

22　處理稅務問題 ·················· *31*

23　問路 ·················· *32*

24　報到 ·················· *33*

25　報到 ⑴ ·················· *34*

26　行李太大／太重 ⑴ ·················· *35*

27　行李遺失／毀損 ·················· *36*

28　去飯店 ·················· *37*

Part 4 住房

29　登記住房 ·················· *40*

30　設備出問題 ·················· *41*

31　要求客房服務 ·················· *42*

32　送洗衣服 ·················· *43*

33 付帳 ……………… *44*

34 付帳 ⠀⠀ ……………… *45*

35 帳單有問題 ……………… *46*

36 信用卡有問題 ⠀⠀ ……………… *47*

37 客房點餐 ……………… *48*

38 使用早餐券 ⠀⠀ ……………… *49*

39 餐廳點餐 ⠀⠀ ……………… *50*

40 餐廳點餐 ……………… *51*

Part 5 搭計程車

41 搭計程車 1 ……………… *54*

42 搭計程車 2 ……………… *55*

43 給小費 ……………… *56*

44 和司機閒聊 ……………… *57*

Part 6 觀光和休閒

45 租用交通工具和運動設施 ……………… *60*

46 上賭場 ……………… *61*

47 去博物館／藝廊 ……………… *62*

48 打高爾夫球 ················ *63*

49 相機和底片 ················ *64*

50 買紀念品 ················ *65*

Part 7 變更計畫

51 延長停留時間 ················ *68*

52 沒有空房 �)) ················ *69*

53 更換飯店 ················ *70*

54 更改班機 ················ *71*

55 班機延誤／取消 ················ *72*

56 簽證有問題 ················ *73*

Part 8 突發狀況

57 生病與買藥 ················ *76*

58 受傷與就醫 ················ *77*

59 通報意外 ················ *78*

60 通報失竊 ················ *79*

61 通報重罪 ················ *80*

62 避免被敲竹槓／被騙 ················ *81*

3

Section

洽談業務好用句

Part 9 電話預約會面

63 約時間 …………… *86*

64 確認會面 …………… *87*

65 重訂見面時間 …………… *88*

66 更改見面地點 …………… *89*

67 換人赴約 …………… *90*

68 詢問細節 …………… *91*

Part 10 參加商展

69 如何前往展場 …………… *94*

70 向主辦單位報到 …………… *95*

71 解決問題 1 …………… *96*

72 解決問題 2 …………… *97*

73 向客人自我介紹 …………… *98*

74 介紹他人 ⋯⋯⋯⋯ *99*

75 簡便推銷用語 ⋯⋯⋯⋯ *100*

76 談論產品 ⋯⋯⋯ *101*

77 留住客人 ⋯⋯⋯ *102*

78 送客人樣品 ⋯⋯⋯ *103*

79 交換聯絡方式 1 ⋯⋯⋯⋯ *104*

80 交換聯絡方式 2 ⋯⋯⋯⋯ *105*

81 敲定買賣 1 ⋯⋯⋯⋯ *106*

82 敲定買賣 2 ⋯⋯⋯⋯ *107*

83 買賣條件 ⋯⋯⋯ *108*

84 運送／交付協議 ⋯⋯⋯⋯ *109*

Part 11 出席研討會／產業智庫

85 表達對主題／講者的興趣 ⋯⋯⋯⋯ *112*

86 開場 ⋯⋯⋯⋯ *113*

87 介紹發言人／講者 ⋯⋯⋯ *114*

88 說明時間表和用餐情形 ⋯⋯⋯⋯ *115*

Part 12 參觀工廠

89 表達興趣 ················ *118*

90 表達滿意 ················ *119*

91 表達不滿 1 ················ *120*

92 表達不滿 2 ················ *121*

Part 13 做簡報

93 見面與問候 ················ *124*

94 自我介紹 ················ *125*

95 以數據／資料／統計數字來說明 ················ *126*

96 討論目標 ················ *127*

97 討論研究發現 ················ *128*

98 排除干擾 ················ *129*

99 總結 ················ *130*

100 接受及鼓勵提問 ················ *131*

Part 14 協商合約

101 標準說法 1 ················ *134*

102 標準說法 2 ················ *135*

103 挽回買賣 ·············· *136*

104 合作 ·············· *137*

105 強勢出擊 ·············· *138*

106 保密協定 ·············· *139*

107 詢問進展 ·············· *140*

108 簽約 ·············· *141*

Part 15 交際

109 建議用餐 ·············· *144*

110 建議喝一杯 ·············· *145*

111 建議活動 ·············· *146*

112 接受／婉拒邀約 ·············· *147*

113 點酒 ·············· *148*

114 點餐 ·············· *149*

115 要求服務 ·············· *150*

116 敬酒 ·············· *151*

117 訂位／更改訂位 ·············· *152*

118 訂位／更改訂位 ·············· *153*

119 談公事 ·············· *154*

120 避談公事 ················· *155*

121 請客 ················· *156*

122 搶著付帳 ················· *157*

4
Section

追蹤業務加分句

123 客套用語 ················· *160*

124 寄送資料 ················· *161*

125 繼續／終止生意往來 ················· *162*

126 繼續推銷 ················· *163*

5
Section

出差好用字

127 旅客常見疾病 ················· *166*

128 成藥 ················· *167*

129 飯店設施及服務 ················· *168*

130 餐廳類型 ·················· *169*

131 展館用語 ··············· *170*

132 簡報視聽設備 ················· *171*

133 數字和單位 ··············· *172*

134 錢的相關說法 ················· *173*

附錄 1　國際小費標準 ················· *174*

附錄 2　各國免稅商品額度比較 ·················· *175*

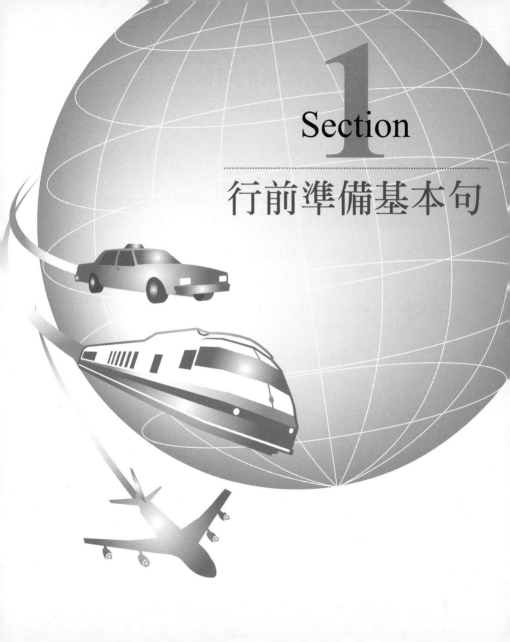

Section

1

行前準備基本句

1 探詢拜會的可能

這些句子適用於電子郵件和電話。

☐ I'm going to be in town.
到時我會在市內。

☐ Would it be possible for me to stop in and see you?
我可以順道去拜訪你嗎？

☐ I'd like to have a look at the warehouse.[1]
我想去倉庫看看。

☐ The boss has asked me to pay you a visit.
老闆要我去拜訪你。

☐ I'd like to drop by[2] and check out the situation.
我想過來看看狀況。

☐ The boss wants me to have a look at the facility[3] for myself.
老闆要我自己去視察一下工廠設備。

Word list

1 warehouse [`wɛr,haʊs] *n.* 倉庫；儲倉室

2 drop by 【口語】（沒有事先通知）拜訪；順道造訪

3 facility [fə`sɪlətɪ] *n.* 設備，設施；（供特定用途的）場所

2 接受 / 確認邀請

這些句子適用於電子郵件和電話。

☐ I just wanted to remind you I'll be in town from the 5th until the 11th.

我只是想提醒你，我從五號到十一號會在市內。

☐ I just wanted to confirm that there will be someone to pick me up at the airport.

我只是想確定，會有人到機場接我。

☐ I'm pleased to accept your invitation.[1]

很高興接受你們的邀請。

☐ I'll be there!

到時候見！

☐ I can't attend personally but Steve will go in my place.[2]

我沒辦法親自出席，不過史提夫會代替我去。

☐ I can't wait to meet you in person![3]

我等不及要見你本人了！

Word list

1 invitation [ˌɪnvəˈteʃən] *n.* 招待；邀請

2 in one's place 代替某人

3 meet sb. in person 會見……本人

3 蒐集商展訊息

☐ How many attendees[1] do you expect?

你預計會有多少人出席？

☐ What was the attendance[2] last year?

去年有多少人出席？

☐ What is the layout[3]/size of the space?

場地規劃如何／有多大？

☐ How long does the show run?

這次展覽會舉行多久？

☐ What is the cost of the space/booth?[4]

這個場地／攤位要多少錢？

☐ What's included in the cost of the space?

場地費包含哪些項目？

Word list

1 attendee [ətɛnˋdi] *n.* 出席者；參加者（＝【美】attendant）

2 attendance [əˋtɛndəns] *n.* 出席者；參加人數（用單數）

3 layout [ˋleˏaʊt] *n.* 規劃；設計

4 booth [buθ] *n.* 攤位；攤子

4 登記參加商展

CD 1 06

☐ How many companies have reserved space so far?

到目前為止有多少公司預訂場地？

☐ Can I register[1] online?

我可以上網登記嗎？

☐ I'd like to reserve a booth/space.

我想要預訂一個攤位／場地。

☐ What methods of payment do you accept?

你們接受哪些付款方式？

☐ Will you give me a confirmation[2] number?

你們會給我確認號碼嗎？

☐ Whom should I contact if I have any questions?

假如有問題的話，我應該和誰聯絡？

Word list
1 register [`rɛdʒɪstɚ] v. （正式地）登記；註冊
2 confirmation [kɑnfɚ`meʃən] n. 確認；認定

5　預訂飯店

☐ I need a single/double room.

我要一間單人 / 雙人房。

☐ Do you have a suite[1] available?[2]

你們有空套房嗎？

☐ The junior suite sounds like a more reasonable deal.

小套房聽起來比較划算。

☐ Please tell me you have rooms available for tomorrow/October 3rd through 5th.

拜託明天 / 十月三號到五號一定有空房。

☐ Please reserve the room for me. My last name is Chen, C-H-E-N. First name, Jack.

請幫我保留這個房間。我姓陳，耳東陳，名字是傑克。

☐ OK, you can go ahead and book the room. My name is Matin Hsieh, H-S-I-E-H.

好，您可以訂房了。我叫馬丁·謝，謝謝的謝。

Word list
[1] suite [swit] *n.* 套房
[2] available [ə`veləbl] *adj.* （物、消息、工作等）可取得的；可得到的；有空的

6 打聽會展的最新消息

☐ Who will attend? Are there any big names[1] going?

有誰會出席？有什麼大人物會去嗎？

☐ Have you been to that convention center before? How is it?

你以前去過那個會議中心嗎？怎麼樣？

☐ What's the occasion?

情況怎麼樣？

☐ Will anybody I know be there?

會有我認識的人去嗎？

☐ Do you think I'd get anything out of it?

你覺得我會有什麼收穫嗎？

☐ I went last year and I got / didn't get a lot out of it.

我去年去了，有／沒有很多收穫。

Word list **1** big name 【口語】 名人；重要的人物

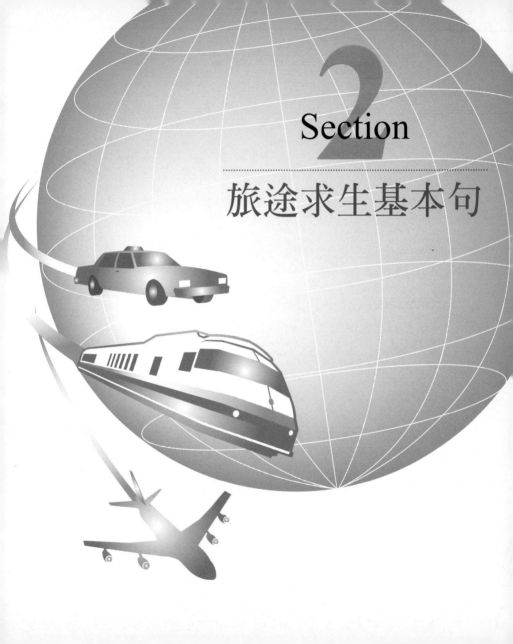

Section 2

旅途求生基本句

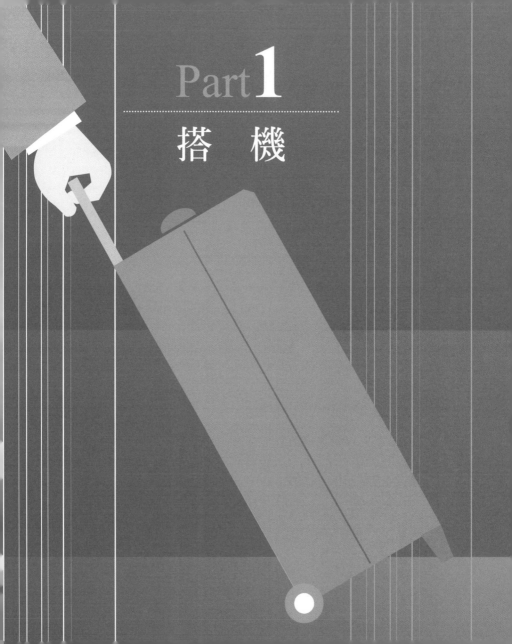

Part**1**

搭　機

7 要求處理行李

這些話可以對空服員和其他乘客說。

☐ I'm sorry to trouble you. Could you help me stow[1] this?

抱歉麻煩你一下。你可以幫我把它塞到上頭嗎？

☐ I can't reach the overhead bin.

我搆不到上面的置物箱。

☐ Please be careful — it's fragile[2]/heavy.

請小心——它很脆弱／重。

☐ Would you mind pushing that bag in my direction?

你介不介意把那個袋子挪往我這個方向？

☐ Would you be good enough to help me get my parcel/bag/valise[3] down?

可不可以麻煩你幫我把包包／袋子／手提箱拿下來？

☐ My bag is upside down! Everything must have shifted during the flight.

我的袋子顛倒了！飛行的時候一定動到裡面的東西了。

Word list

1 stow [sto] *v.* 將（東西）收入；裝進

2 fragile [ˋfrædʒəl] *a.* 易碎的；脆弱的

3 valise [vəˋlis] *n.* 旅行用手提包

8 要求換位子

CD1 10

請空服員幫你安排。這些話在辦理登機手續時也用得上。

☐ I'd prefer a window/an aisle¹ seat.

我想要靠窗／靠走道的位子。

☐ I'd rather not sit so close to the toilets.

我不想坐得靠廁所這麼近。

☐ Can I sit at the back of the plane?

我可以坐在機艙的尾端嗎？

☐ Would it be possible to assign me a seat with more legroom?²

可以幫我劃個放腳空間較大的位子嗎？

☐ Those kids are out of control. I can't get any work done where I'm sitting.

這些孩子很野。我在位子上根本沒辦法做事。

☐ I have a medical condition. I can't sit next to the emergency³ exit.

我有特殊的病況。我不能坐在緊急出口的旁邊。

Word list

1 aisle [aɪl] *n.* （劇院、火車或飛機座位中的縱直）通道

2 legroom [ˋlɛɡˌrum] *n.* （劇院、火車或飛機座位前的）伸腳空間

3 emergency [ɪˋmɝdʒənsɪ] *n.* 緊急；危急

9 要求升等

☐ I'm a member of your VIP Club. Any chance of moving up to first class?

我是你們 VIP 俱樂部的會員。有機會升級到頭等艙嗎？

☐ I'd like to upgrade[1] to business class.

我想升等到商務艙。

☐ When I asked on the phone, I was told I could upgrade onboard.[2]

我在電話裡詢問的時候，我被告知，我可以在飛機上升等。

☐ I think there's been a mistake. I never fly economy class.

我想你們搞錯了。我從來不搭經濟艙。

☐ I was told I had a seat reserved in business class.[3]

我被告知說，商務艙有保留位子給我。

☐ I was guaranteed a seat in first class.

他們保證我在頭等艙有座位。

Word list

1 upgrade [`ʌp`gred] v. 使升級；升等
2 onboard [`ɑn`bord] adv. 在交通工具上
3 economy class [ɪ`kɑnəmɪ ˌklæs] n. 經濟艙

10 要求協助填寫出入境表格 CD 12

☐ Sir/Miss, could I borrow a pen?
先生 / 小姐，我可以借個筆嗎？

☐ What is this box asking exactly?
這格到底要填什麼？

☐ Could you tell me our flight number?
麻煩你告訴我班機編號好嗎？

☐ I don't speak Spanish. Can you tell me what this means?
我不會說西班牙話。麻煩你告訴我這是什麼意思好嗎？

☐ Is this asking for my nationality/passport number?
這是不是在問我的國籍 / 護照號碼？

☐ Could you tell me the duty-free limit on alcohol and tobacco?
麻煩你告訴我菸酒的免稅規定好嗎？

Word list
1 nationality [ˌnæʃə`nælətɪ] *n.* 國籍
2 tobacco [tə`bæko] *n.* （有別於香煙或雪茄的）菸草類商品

11 要求服務

☐ I'd like some headphones/a pillow/a blanket,[1] please.

我想要一副耳機 / 一個枕頭 / 一張毯子，麻煩你。

☐ I'd like to purchase some items from duty-free.

我想要買一些免稅商品。

☐ I'd like a bottle of the Merlot. It's number 248 in the catalog.

我想要一瓶 Merlot 紅酒。它在目錄上的號碼是 248。

☐ I'd like a carton[2] of cigarettes, please — Dunhills.

我想要一條 Dunhills 香菸，麻煩你。

☐ I want to buy some perfume — Scarlet Fire — the three-ounce bottle.

我想要買一瓶三盎司裝的 Scarlet Fire 香水。

☐ Could I get another drink/a snack?[3]

我可以再來一杯 / 一份點心嗎？

Word list
1 blanket [ˋblæŋkɪt] *n.* 毛毯
2 carton [ˋkɑrtṇ] *n.* 硬紙盒；厚紙箱
3 snack [snæk] *n.* （三餐以外的）點心

12 要求轉機

☐ How long is our layover?[1]

我們中途要暫停多久？

☐ Do we need to change planes?

我們需要轉機嗎？

☐ Is my baggage checked all the way through to Bangkok?

我的行李會一路被託運到曼谷嗎？

☐ What do you mean I can't get off the plane?

你說我不能下飛機是什麼意思？

☐ Can you tell me where I catch my connecting flight?

麻煩你告訴我要去哪裡轉機好嗎？

☐ I'm going to stroll[2] around the airport for a while. What time is my next flight?

我要去機場逛一下。下一班飛機是什麼時候？

Word
list
1 layover [`le,ovɚ] *n.* 中途停留

2 stroll [strol] *v.* 溜達；閒逛

Part2

驗照與通關

13　驗照))

☐ Q₁ : Destination?[1]

　　目的地？

☐ Q₂ : Where will you be staying while in Canada?

　　你在加拿大的時候會待在什麼地方？

☐ Q₃ : Do you know the address?

　　你知道地址嗎？

☐ Q₄ : Please look into the camera.

　　請看著鏡頭。

☐ Q₅ : How long were you in Germany?

　　你在德國待了多久？

☐ Q₆ : What's the purpose of your visit to the United States?

　　你來美國的目的是什麼？

Word list
❶ destination [ˌdɛstəˋneʃən] *n.* 目的地

14 驗照

☐ A₁： Philadelphia, and then Chicago.
費城，然後是芝加哥。

☐ A₂： The Pan Pacific Vancouver.
溫哥華泛太平洋飯店。

☐ A₃： Just a moment. Let me get the address.
稍等一下。我看看地址。

☐ A₄： Here is a copy of my itinerary.[1]
這是我的行程。

☐ A₅： I was there fourteen days.
我在那裡待了十四天。

☐ A₆： Business. I'm attending[2] a trade show and some meetings at our branch office.[3]
洽公。我要來參加商展，還要到我們的分公司開會。

Word list
[1] itinerary [aɪ`tɪnə,rɛrɪ] *n.* 旅行計畫；行程表
[2] attend [ə`tɛnd] *v.* 列席（會議）；參加（儀式）
[3] branch office [`bræntʃ ,ɔfɪs] *n.* 分公司

15 申報繳稅物品與檢疫 🔊

☐ Do you have anything to declare?[1]

你有什麼東西要申報的嗎？

☐ The green lane is for passengers with nothing to declare.

沒有東西要申報的旅客請走綠色通道。

☐ Sorry sir/ma'am, you're over the limit for bottled spirits[2]/ cigarettes.

抱歉，先生 / 小姐，你的瓶裝酒 / 菸超出規定了。

☐ You can't bring that/those into the country.

你不能帶這個 / 這些入境。

☐ Your dog/cat will have to be placed in quarantine.[3]

你的狗 / 貓必須接受檢疫。

☐ Importing fruit is prohibited.[4]

水果不可以帶進來。

Word list
1 declare [dɪ`klɛr] v. （在海關、稅務機構）申報（繳稅物品）
2 spirit [`spɪrɪt] n. 烈酒
3 quarantine [`kwɔrən͵tin] n. 隔離；檢疫
4 prohibited [prə`hɪbɪtɪd] adj. 禁止的

16 申報繳稅物品與檢疫

☐ No, I don't. / Yes, I do. Here's my form.

沒有／有。這是我的申報表。

☐ Which lane should I go through?

我應該走哪一條通道？

☐ Is that so. What is the limit?

是嗎。規定是多少？

☐ I have a permit,[1] though. Take a look.

可是我有許可證。你看。

☐ Quarantine? For how long? It's a sample for the trade show I'm going to.

檢疫？要多久？這是我要帶去商展的樣品。

☐ I'm sorry. My little girl must have put that (apple) in there when I wasn't looking.

抱歉。我的小女兒一定是趁我不注意的時候把它（蘋果）放進來了。

Word list **1** permit [ˋpɝmɪt] *n.* 許可證

17 違反規定)))

☐ Mind if I have a look in your bag?

介意我看看你的袋子裡頭嗎？

☐ You can have a seat over here, please?

可以麻煩你在這邊坐一下嗎？

☐ Did you pack this bag yourself, sir/ma'am?

先生 / 小姐，這個袋子是你自己打包的嗎？

☐ Are you aware that it's illegal[1] to import items of this nature?

你知道帶這種東西進來是違法的嗎？

☐ You're liable[2] to pay the duty[3] on these items.

這些東西你必須繳稅。

☐ You can pay at that counter over there. Go see that man/woman.

你可以去那邊的那個櫃檯繳費。找那位男士 / 女士。

Word list
1 illegal [ɪˋligl] *adj.* 違法的；不合法的
2 liable [ˋlaɪəbl] *adj.* 應負責的；有責任的
3 duty [ˋdutɪ] *n.* 稅；關稅

18 違反規定

超出規定或發生更糟的狀況時,可用這些句子。

☐ No. Go right ahead.

沒關係。儘管看吧。

☐ Of course not. Let me get the lock for you.

當然不會。我來幫你把鎖打開。

☐ Sorry, I can't seem to find the key. Just a second.

抱歉,我似乎找不到鑰匙。稍等一下。

☐ Hey, how did that get in there?

咦,它怎麼會在裡面?

☐ Illegal? No, I wasn't aware of that.

違法?不,我不知道。

☐ I don't have any cash on my person. Can I use a credit card?

我身上沒有帶現金。我可以用信用卡嗎?

19 遇上大麻煩 🔊

這些問句希望你永遠不會聽到。

☐ This is very serious business.
這件事很嚴重。

☐ The government of Malaysia takes smuggling[1] very seriously.
馬來西亞政府對走私管得很嚴。

☐ You're being placed under arrest.[2]
你被逮捕了。

☐ Perhaps you should contact a lawyer.
也許你應該找一位律師。

☐ You're entitled[3] to a phone call.
你可以打電話。

☐ You'll have to give the officer your valuables,[4] your belt, and your shoelaces.
你必須把你的貴重物品、腰帶和鞋帶拿給警官。

Word list
1 smuggle [`smʌgl] v. 把……走私運入;把……偷帶進
2 under arrest 被逮捕
3 entitle [ɪn`taɪtl] v. 給……權利(資格)做……(常用被動語態)
4 valuable [`væljʊəbl] n. 貴重物(常用複數)

20 遇上大麻煩

若不幸遇上這些大麻煩，需要救兵可使用下列句子。

☐ Is there a problem?
有問題嗎？

☐ I think I'm going to need a Chinese interpreter.[1]
我想我需要一位華語翻譯。

☐ TECRO needs to be notified immediately.
我要立刻通知台北經濟文化代表處。

☐ I need a Chinese-speaking lawyer.
我需要一位會講中文的律師。

☐ May I ask why I'm being detained?[2]
我可以問一下我為什麼被拘留嗎？

☐ I need to contact my company's branch office here. May I make a phone call?
我要聯絡我在這裡的分公司。我可以打個電話嗎？

Word list
1 interpreter [ɪn`tɝprɪtɚ] *n.* 翻譯者（官）
2 detain [dɪ`ten] *v.* 拘留；扣押

Part *2* 驗照與通關

Part3

在機場

21 換錢

☐ I need to exchange some money.
我要換一點錢。

☐ Where can I exchange currency?[1]
我可以去哪裡換匯？

☐ What's the exchange rate?
匯率是多少？

☐ Can I use U.S. dollars/Euros here?
這裡可以用美元／歐元嗎？

☐ I'd like to convert[2] this to Renminbi.[3]
我想把這個換成人民幣。

☐ I want to buy 1,500 Euros, please.
我想要買一千五百歐元，麻煩你。

Word list

1 currency [`kɝənsɪ] *n.* 通貨；貨幣

2 convert [kən`vɝt] *v.* 兌換；換算

3 renminbi [`rɛn`mɪn`bi] *n.* 人民幣（中華人民共和國貨幣）

22

處理稅務問題

CD1 24

每個國家對加值稅與機場／離境稅的規定不盡相同，出發前可先上網查詢相關訊息。

申請退還加值稅

☐ Are foreign visitors eligible[1] for a Value Added Tax (VAT) refund?

外國遊客有資格退還加值稅嗎？

☐ I need the form to claim[2] the VAT tax refund.

我需要表格來申請退還加值稅。

☐ I have receipts[3] for everything.

每樣東西我都有收據。

繳交離境／機場稅

☐ Where do I pay the departure/airport tax?

我要去哪裡繳離境／機場稅？

☐ Is the departure/airport tax payable[4] in U.S. dollars?

離境／機場稅可以用美元繳嗎？

☐ I forgot I needed local currency for the departure/airport tax. Where's there a bank machine?

我忘了得用本地貨幣來繳離境／機場稅。哪裡有櫃員機？

Word list

1. eligible [`ɛlɪdʒəbḷ] *adj.* 適合做……的；有資格作……的
2. claim [klem] *v.* 要求；請求（權利、遺產）
3. receipt [rɪ`sit] *n.* 收據；收條
4. payable [`peəbḷ] *adj.* 可支付的；付得起的

23 | 問路

☐ In which direction is Gate 33?

三十三號登機門在哪個方向？

☐ Could you direct me to the China Airlines check-in counter?

你可以告訴我中華航空的報到櫃台要怎麼走？

☐ Which way to the baggage claim area?

行李提領區要怎麼走？

☐ Where would I find a smoking lounge[1]/ATM machine around here?

這附近哪裡有吸菸室／自動櫃員機？

☐ Am I in the right terminal for my flight? It's KLM flight 877 to Taipei.

我是在對的航站嗎？我坐荷航八七七號班機飛往台北。

☐ How do I get to terminal two?

二號航站要怎麼走？

Word
list
　　1 lounge [laundʒ] *n.* （有化妝室、吸煙室的）休憩室
　　2 terminal [ˋtɝmɪnl] *n.* （機場的）航空站

24 報到

☐ I was told I am waitlisted[1] for this flight. Are any seats available?

我被告知可以候補這班飛機。還有空位嗎？

☐ I have an electronic ticket.

我有電子機票。

☐ I would like to upgrade my seat.

我想要升等座位。

☐ Do I need to confirm my connecting flight(s)?

我需要確認我的轉接班機嗎？

☐ I have two bags to check and one carry-on.[2]

我有兩個袋子要託運和一件隨身行李。

☐ Is this small enough to carry on?

這種大小可以隨身攜帶嗎？

Word
list

1 waitlist [`wet͵lɪst] v. 把……登記於補位（候補）名單上

2 carry-on [`kærɪ͵ɑn] n. （旅客帶入機艙內的）隨身手提行李 /
adj. 可身攜帶的

☐ Could I have your ticket and your passport, please?

可以麻煩你把機票和護照拿出來嗎？

☐ Do you prefer window or aisle?

你要靠窗還是靠走道？

☐ Will you be checking any bags with us today?

你今天有行李要託運嗎？

☐ Sir/Ma'am, I suggest you fill out a nametag and put it on your bag, just in case.[1]

先生／小姐，我建議你寫個名牌掛在袋子上，以防萬一。

☐ Here's your boarding pass.[2]

這是你的登機證。

☐ You'll be boarding at Gate 88-D. Boarding time is 11:30.

你要在 88-D 門登機。登機時間是十一點半。

Word list
1 just in case【口語】以防萬一
2 boarding pass [ˋbordɪŋ ˏpæs] *n.* 登機證

26 行李太大 / 太重 🎧

☐ I'm sorry, but your bags are over the weight allowance.[1] The limit is 20 kilos per person.

抱歉，你的行李超重了。上限是每個人二十公斤。

☐ There's a surcharge[2] of eight dollars per kilogram on over-weight baggage.

超重的行李每公斤加收八元。

☐ I'm sorry, that won't fit in the overhead bins. You'll have to check it.

抱歉，這放不進上面的置物箱，你必須託運。

☐ You're (only) allowed one piece of carry-on luggage.

你（只）可以帶一件隨身行李。

☐ Sorry, sir/ma'am, but that's our policy.

抱歉，先生 / 小姐，這是我們的規定。

☐ Let me call/get my supervisor.

我請／找我的主管來。

Word list
1 allowance [ə`lauəns] *n.* 限額；定量
2 surcharge [`sɝ͵tʃɑrdʒ] *n.* 附加費；追加的費用

27 行李遺失 / 毀損

袋子遺失與受損是很麻煩的事，不幸發生時你可以這樣說。

☐ My bags haven't shown up/were damaged/were delayed.

我的袋子不見 / 受損 / 被耽擱了。

☐ My luggage never arrived/was damaged/has been delayed.

我的行李根本沒來 / 受損了 / 被耽擱了。

☐ Items have been stolen from my bag.

我的袋子裡有東西被偷了。

☐ Where can I go to lodge[1] a complaint against the airline?

我要去哪裡申訴航空公司？

☐ You can see the damage for yourself.

你可以自己看看受損的情況。

☐ Your airline is clearly responsible (for this). What compensation[2] can I expect?

你們航空公司必須（為這件事）負責。我能得到什麼樣的賠償？

Word list

1 lodge [lɑdʒ] v. 呈遞（訴狀、申告書等）

2 compensation [ˌkɑmpənˈseʃən] n. 補償；賠償

28 去飯店

☐ Where is the taxi stand?[1]

計程車招呼站在哪裡？

☐ Where can I get a cab/shuttle bus?[2]

我要去哪裡搭計程車／接駁公車？

☐ Is there a shuttle bus to downtown/to the major hotels?

有去市中心／大飯店的接駁公車嗎？

☐ I'm meeting someone in the arrivals (parking) lot. Where's
that?

我要在入境室（停車場）跟人會面。那在什麼地方？

☐ Someone from the company should be waiting for me in the
arrivals lounge.

公司的人應該會在入境室等我。

☐ Can you tell me where to go to rent a car?

可以告訴我要到哪裡租車嗎？

Word
list

1 stand [stænd] *n.* （計程車的）招呼站

2 shuttle bus [`ʃʌtḷ ˌbʌs] *n.* 接駁車；定期往返的公車

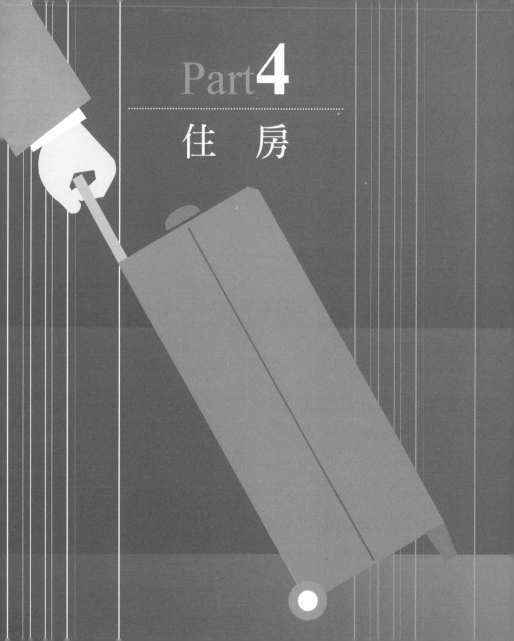

Part**4**

住　房

29 登記住房

☐ I have a reservation under Huang.
我有訂房，我姓黃。

☐ I have a reservation[1] — surname,[2] Wang.
我有訂房，我姓王。

☐ I need to check in. My name is Sean Lee.
我要辦住房手續。我叫尚‧李。

☐ Is my room ready yet? Can I check in early?
我的房間準備好了嗎？我可以早點住進去嗎？

☐ I'm too early? What time is check-in?
我太早來了嗎？什麼時候可以住進去？

☐ What time is check-out?
什麼時候要退房？

Word list
1 reservation [ˌrɛzɚˋveʃən] *n.* 預約；預訂
2 surname [ˋsɝˌnem] *n.* 姓

30 設備出問題

☐ There's a strange/musty[1] smell.
　裡面有股奇怪 / 發霉的味道。

☐ I requested a non-smoking room.
　我要一間非吸菸室。

☐ There's an annoying sound coming from the ceiling fan.
　吊扇的聲音很吵。

☐ The refrigerator isn't working.
　冰箱壞了。

☐ There seems to be a problem with the cable/water pressure/toilet/shower.
　第四台 / 水壓 / 馬桶 / 淋浴器好像有問題。

☐ Can you send someone up to have a look?
　你能找人來看看嗎？

Word list **1** musty [ˋmʌstɪ] *adj.* 霉臭的；發霉的

31 要求客房服務

☐ I'd like to arrange a wake-up call for six-thirty.

我想設定六點半的起床呼叫。

☐ I need to send this fax. It's urgent!

我要發這份傳真，而且很緊急！

☐ I'd like to work out.[1] Where's the gym?[2]

我想去健身。健身房在哪裡？

☐ Do you offer photocopying[3] service?

你們有提供影印服務嗎？

☐ Where can I access[4] the Internet? Do you have wireless access?

哪裡可以上網？你們有無線上網嗎？

☐ Could you call a taxi for me, please?

可以麻煩你幫我叫計程車嗎？

Word list

1 work out 健身；運動

2 gym [dʒɪm] *n.* 【口語】健身房

3 photocopy [ˋfotəˏkɑpɪ] *v.* 影印

4 access [ˋæksɛs] *v.* 使用；接近

32 送洗衣服

大部分的飯店都有提供貼心的洗衣服務。

☐ I'd like these clothes laundered,[1] please.

我想送洗這些衣服，麻煩你。

☐ I need these shirts and slacks[2] dry-cleaned and pressed.

我這些襯衫和長褲要乾洗和燙平。

☐ No starch[3] in the shirts, please.

麻煩襯衫不要漿。

☐ This is / these are silk — please be careful with it/them.

這 / 這些是絲質的衣服，麻煩小心處理。

☐ There's a stain[4] here. Please see if you can get it out.

這裡有個污點，麻煩你看看能不能把它弄掉。

☐ I need these back by tomorrow.

這些（衣服）我明天就要。

Word list

1 launder [ˈlɔndɚ] *v.* 洗；洗熨

2 slack [slæk] *n.* 長褲；便褲

3 starch [stɑrtʃ] *n.* （漿衣服的）漿

4 stain [sten] *n.* 污漬；污點

33 付帳

☐ I'll be paying in cash/by credit card.

我要用現金 / 信用卡付款。

☐ Please charge it to my credit card.

請用我的信用卡支付。

☐ Put it (all) on my card, please.

（全部）用我的卡來付，麻煩你。

☐ Do you take Amex/Mastercard/Visa?

你們接受美國運通卡 / 萬士達卡 / 威士卡嗎？

☐ Can I cash[1] traveler's cheques[2] here?

這裡可以兌現旅行支票嗎？

☐ Would it be possible to pay by debit card?[3]

可以用簽帳卡付款嗎？

Word list

1 cash [kæʃ] v. 把（支票或票據）兌現

2 traveler's cheque [ˋtrævls ˏtʃɛk] n. 旅行支票 (= traveler's check)

3 debit card [ˋdɛbɪt ˏkɑrd] n. 簽帳卡

34 付帳))♪

☐ How will you be paying, sir/ma'am?

先生／小姐，你要怎麼付款？

☐ That will be $1,876.75, please.

總共是一八七六‧七五元，麻煩你。

☐ The grand[1] total is $1876.75.

加起來是一八七六‧七五元。

☐ I just need a minute to run your card through.

我需要刷一下你的卡。

☐ Thank you for choosing Radisson Hotels.

謝謝光臨瑞迪森飯店。

☐ I hope you enjoyed your stay.

希望你住得還愉快。

Word
list
1 grand [grænd] *adj.* 包含全部的；總括的

35 帳單有問題

CD1 37

☐ There must be some mistake.

一定有地方搞錯了。

☐ Clearly there has been a mistake.

這顯然是搞錯了。

☐ I certainly didn't make those calls.

我確定沒有打這些電話。

☐ I'm not paying for movies I didn't watch/alcohol I didn't drink.

我不會為我沒有看的電影 / 我沒有喝的酒付錢。

☐ That curtain rod[1]/window was already damaged. I had nothing to do with it![2]

這個窗簾桿 / 窗子早就壞了。我可沒有動它！

☐ I think I should be entitled[3] to some kind of discount. Where's the manager?

我想我應該享有某種折扣。經理在哪裡？

Word list

1 rod [rɑd] *n.* 桿子；棒子

2 have nothing to do with sth. 跟……一點關係也沒有

3 entitle [ɪn`taɪtl] *v.* 有權利（資格）

36 信用卡有問題 CD1 38

這種情形很尷尬，但有時候就是會發生。它當然也可能在飯店以外的地方發生，此時你就要有所準備。

你可能會聽到

☐ Sorry, sir/ma'am. The transaction[1] won't go through.

抱歉，先生 / 小姐，刷卡沒有成功。

☐ There's a problem with your card.

你的卡有問題。

☐ Your card is over the limit/expired.[2]

你的卡刷爆 / 過期了。

你可以說

☐ Impossible. Please try it again.

不可能。麻煩再試試看。

☐ That's strange. Let's try another card instead.

奇怪了。那刷另一張卡好了。

☐ Sorry about that. I gave you the wrong one.

不好意思。我拿錯卡給你了。

Word
list
1 transaction [træn`sækʃən] *n.* （業務的）處理；辦理；執行
2 expire [ɪk`spaɪr] *v.* （期限等）屆滿、終止；（權利等）消失

37 客房點餐

你可能會聽到

☐ Room Service. May I help you?

客房服務。我可以為你效勞嗎？

☐ May I have your room number, please?

可以麻煩你把房間號碼告訴我嗎？

你可能會說

☐ This is room four-twenty (420). I'd like to order some food.

這裡是四二○號房。我想點一些吃的。

☐ Are you still serving meals?

你們還有供餐嗎？

☐ Please bring me a fruit platter[1] and a newspaper.

請給我一份水果盤和一份報紙。

☐ I just want something light.[2] What do you recommend?

我只要一點清淡的東西。你們有什麼可以推薦的嗎？

Word list
1 platter [ˈplætɚ] *n.* 大盤子
2 light [laɪt] *adj.* （食物）易消化的；清淡的；不油膩的

38 使用早餐券))

☐ All our guests are entitled to a free breakfast as part of your stay.

我們的客人只要住房，就可以享用免費的早餐。

☐ Here's your breakfast voucher[1]/coupon.[2]

這是你的早餐券。

☐ Just give them this voucher at the restaurant.

只要把這張券交給餐廳的人就行了。

☐ We serve breakfast starting at 6:30.

我們從六點半開始供應早餐。

☐ Breakfast finishes at 11:00.

早餐供應到十一點為止。

☐ Our complimentary[3] breakfast is buffet-style.[4]

我們附贈的早餐是自助式的。

Word list

1 voucher [ˋvautʃɚ] *n.* 商品交換憑單；商品交換券

2 coupon [ˋkupɑn] *n.* 折扣券；食品交換券

3 complimentary [ˌkɑmpləˋmɛntərɪ] *adj.* （表示好意或敬意之）贈送的

4 buffet-style [buˋfe ˌstaɪl] *adj.* 自助餐式的

☐ Q₁：Something to start?／Care for[1] an appetizer?[2]

要先來點什麼嗎？／想來點開胃菜嗎？

☐ Q₂：Can I get anyone something to drink?

有人要喝點什麼嗎？

☐ Q₃：Would you like soup or salad?

你想要湯還是沙拉？

☐ Q₄：Our specials are grilled[3] sole in lemon sauce, teriyaki[4] beef, or vegetable lasagna[5]. All are served with steamed[6] vegetables.

我們的特餐有檸檬醬烤比目魚、日式烤牛肉或蔬菜寬麵，而且全部附有清蒸蔬菜。

☐ Q₅：You have your choice of baked potato, French fries, or rice pilaf.[7]

你可以選擇烤洋芋、薯條或炒飯。

☐ Q₆：Anyone care for coffee or desert?

有人要咖啡或甜點嗎？

Word
list
1 care for sth. 喜歡……；想要……
2 appetizer [ˈæpəˌtaɪzɚ] *n.* 開胃菜
3 grilled [grɪld] *adj.* 燒烤的
4 teriyaki beef [ˌtɛrɪˈjɑkɪ ˈbif] 日式烤牛肉（在日式沾醬醃泡過再烤）
5 lasagna [ləˈzɑnjə] *n.* （義大利式）滷汁寬麵條
6 steamed [stimd] *adj.* 清蒸的
7 rice pilaf [ˈraɪs ˈpɪlɑf] *n.* 調味炒飯

40 餐廳點餐

□ A₁ : For an appetizer, I'd like the escargot.¹

我想要點蝸牛當開胃菜。

□ A₂ : A glass of the house red,² please.

麻煩來一杯紅餐酒。

□ A₃ : Salad. What dressings³ do you have?

沙拉。你們有什麼醬料？

□ A₄ : What are today's specials?

今天的特餐是什麼？

□ A₅ : I'd like the T-bone steak,⁴ medium,⁵ with a baked potato. Can I get the sour cream⁶ and butter on the side, please?

我想要丁骨牛排，五分熟，加上焗烤洋芋。可以麻煩你酸乳酪醬和奶油放旁邊嗎？

□ A₆ : Sure. Can we see the dessert menu, please?

好啊。麻煩可以讓我們看一下甜點的菜單嗎？

Word list

1 escargot [ˈɛskɑrˌgo] *n.* 食用蝸牛
2 house red [ˈhaʊs ˌrɛd] *n.* 紅餐酒
3 dressing [ˈdrɛsɪŋ] *n.*（澆在生菜沙拉上的）調味醬

4 T-bone steak [ˈtiˌbon ˈstek] *n.* 丁骨牛排
5 medium [ˈmidɪəm] *adj.* 五分熟的
6 sour cream [ˈsaʊr ˈkrim] *n.* 酸乳酪醬

Part 5

搭計程車

41 搭計程車 1

你可能會聽到

☐ Where to? / Where can I take you?
要去哪？／我要載你去哪裡？

你可能會說

☐ Please take me to the Grand Hotel.
請載我去圓山飯店。

☐ I'm going to this address. (hand driver the address)
我要去這個地址。（把地址拿給司機）

☐ The Convention Center, please.
麻煩去會議中心。

☐ Would you mind slowing down?
你可以開慢一點嗎？

☐ I'm running late. Could you step on it?[1]
我快遲到了。你可以開快一點嗎？

Word list ❶ step on it【口語】踩（汽車）油門；加快速度

42 搭計程車 2

☐ You're lost? Don't you have a map?

你迷路了嗎？你沒有地圖嗎？

☐ I need to stop at an ATM[1]/convenience store on the way.

我要在自動櫃員機／便利商店停一下車。

☐ I'll get out here. / Right here is fine.

我要在這裡下車。／在這裡停就可以了。

☐ Can you let me out on the other side of the intersection,[2] please?

麻煩可以讓我在十字路口的另一邊下車嗎？

☐ Keep going straight. Then turn left/right.

往前直走，然後左／右轉。

☐ Can you pop[3] the trunk for me?

你可以幫我打開行李廂嗎？

Word list
1 ATM *n.* 自動櫃員機（= Automated-teller machine）
2 intersection [ˌɪntɚˋsɛkʃən] *n.* （道路的）交叉點；十字路口
3 pop [pɑp] *v.* （突然地、迅速地）移動或打開

凡是遇到要給小費的時候，像是給服務生、導遊、侍者等等，這些話就很有用。

☐ That's for you.

這個給你。

☐ Keep the change.

零錢不用找了。

☐ For your troubles …

麻煩你了……

☐ Don't worry about the change.

不必找零了。

☐ I don't need change.

零錢不必給我了。

☐ Keep five bucks for yourself.

你拿五塊錢給自己吧。

Word list **1** buck [bʌk] *n.*【美俚】一美元

44 和司機閒聊

有時候計程車司機很喜歡聊天。天氣、政治、運動還有你從哪裡來都是常見的話題。

☐ Yes, I'm from out of town. I'm from Taiwan.

對，我是從外地來的。我是從台灣來的。

☐ The weather sure has been beautiful/lousy.[1]

天氣真的很棒 / 很差。

☐ I'm afraid I don't know much about the local political situation.
What's your take?[2]

恐怕我不太了解當地的政治情勢。你有什麼看法？

☐ I don't really follow[3] sports closely.

我其實不太注意體育消息。

☐ Really? That's interesting.

真的嗎？還挺有趣的。

☐ I didn't quite catch[4] that. You said …?

我不太懂意思。你是說……？

Word
list

1 lousy [ˋlauzɪ] *a.* 討厭的；很糟的；令人作嘔的

2 take [tek] *n.* 反應；看法

3 follow [ˋfɑlo] *v.* 感興趣地注意……；關注……

4 catch [kætʃ] *v.* 聽懂；了解

Section *2* 旅途求生基本句   **57**

Part6

觀光與休閒

45　租用交通工具和運動設施　CD1 47

□ I wish to rent a bike/moped¹/jet ski.

我想租腳踏車 / 機器腳踏車 / 噴氣式滑雪板。

□ How much for one hour/day?

一小時 / 一天要多少錢？

□ Does the rental² include insurance?³

租金包含保險嗎？

□ When does it need to be back?

什麼時候要還？

□ There's a problem with this one. Can you give me another?

這個有點問題。可以給我另一個嗎？

□ I've never ridden/driven/used one before. I need some instruction.⁴

我以前從來沒騎過 / 開過 / 用過。我需要一點指點。

Word list

1 moped [ˋmopɛd] *n.* 機器腳踏車
2 rental [ˋrɛntl] *n.* 租金總額；租約
3 insurance [ɪnˋʃurəns] *n.* 保險；保險業
4 instruction [ɪnˋstrʌkʃən] *n.* 指示；指令

46 上賭場

☐ I'm not much of a gambler.[1]

我不太會賭。

☐ Gambling's in my blood!

我愛賭得不得了！

☐ I'm going to cash[2] in my chips.

我要去兌現我的籌碼。

☐ I won/lost big.

我贏／輸了一大筆。

☐ I was on a roll![3]/I almost lost my shirt!

我手氣很旺！／我幾乎連褲子都輸掉了！

☐ Hit[4] me!/I fold![5]/Call.[6]/I'll raise you 10.

發牌！／不玩了！／跟牌。／我要加注十塊。

Word
list

1 gambler [`gæmblɚ] *n.* 賭徒；好賭之人；
投機商人

2 cash [kæʃ] *v.* （在賭場）把籌碼變成現金

3 on a roll 處於連續的好運或成功之中

4 hit [hɪt] *v.*【口語】丟過來

5 fold [fold] *v.*【口語】不玩了

6 call [kɔl] *v.*【紙牌】請求出牌或攤牌

47 去博物館／藝廊

你可能會聽到

☐ This piece dates from[1] the eleventh century.
這件作品可以追溯到十一世紀。

☐ This vase is a fine example of...
這個花瓶是……的好例子。

☐ This painting is typical[2] of Van Gogh's later work. Notice the bold strokes[3] and colors.
這幅畫是梵谷後期的典型作品。注意它大膽的線條與色彩。

你可能會說

☐ It's magnificent.[4]
真了不起。

☐ The workmanship is exquisite.[5] Imagine how long it must have taken to craft[6] it.
做工真細。可想而知它花了多久的時間才做出來。

☐ I can't get over the attention to detail.
我想不注意到小地方都很難。

Word list

1 date from …從…開始

2 typical [ˋtɪpɪk!] *adj.* 代表…的；象徵…的

3 stroke [strok] *n.* 筆法；一筆；一刀

4 magnificent [mægˋnɪfəsənt] *adj.* 極美的；很動人的

5 exquisite [ˋɛkskwɪzɪt] *adj.* 精美的；絕妙的

6 craft [kræft] *v.*【美】精巧地製作

48 打高爾夫球

CD1 50

除了說「漂亮的揮桿」和「漂亮的推桿」之類的話以外，你還可以在去球場會館的酒吧前試試這些話。

☐ Let's hit the links. Do we need to reserve a tee[1] time?

我們去打高爾夫球吧。我們需要跟球場預約時間嗎？

☐ I want to hit some balls at a driving range.[2] Is there one nearby?

我想去練習場打打球。這附近有球場嗎？

☐ I'm a seven handicap.[3]

我的差點是七。

☐ Want to walk or rent a cart?

想走路還是租車？

☐ I'm keen to take a lesson. How much for an hour with a pro?[4]

我很想多學一點。和職業選手打一小時要多少錢？

☐ Oh, no! I'm in the water/sand/rough![5]

噢，不會吧！我進水池 / 沙坑 / 長草了！

Word list

1 tee [ti] *n.* 高爾夫球

2 driving range [`draɪvɪŋ `rendʒ] *n.* 【高爾夫】練習場

3 handicap [`hændɪ͵kæp] *n.* 【運動】差

點；差距（高爾夫比賽為優待功力不如者自其實際桿數扣除某一數目之桿數）

4 pro [pro] *n.* 【口語】職業選手；專家；行家

5 rough [`rʌf] *n.* 【高爾夫球】深草區

49 相機和底片

☐ I need to charge[1] my battery.

我的電池要充電了。

☐ Shit! I forgot to pack my charger![2]

媽的！我忘了帶充電器！

☐ I need to pick up a roll of film/a memory card/some batteries.

我要去買一捲底片／一張記憶卡／一些電池。

☐ I need to get this film developed.[3]

我要去沖洗這捲底片。

☐ I'd like to order prints/slides of this roll.

我想把這捲洗成照片／幻燈片。

☐ Is it safe to put film through the x-ray machine?

底片經過 X 光機安全嗎？

Word list

1 charge [tʃɑrdʒ] v. 將……充電

2 charger [`tʃɑrdʒɚ] n. 充電器

3 develop [dɪ`vɛləp] v. 【攝影】顯像

50 買紀念品

☐ I can't go home empty-handed.

我可不能空手而回。

☐ I'm looking for something distinctive[1]/original to remember my trip.

我要找個特別 / 獨一無二的東西來紀念我的旅程。

☐ The souvenir[2] shop is overpriced/a rip off![3]

這家紀念品販賣店賣得太貴了 / 簡直是在坑人！

☐ These souvenirs are so tacky.[4]

這些紀念品太俗了。

☐ That isn't/wasn't exactly what I had in mind. Can you show me something else?

那根本不是我想要的東西。你們可以給我看點別的嗎？

☐ No, the last thing I need is another t-shirt.

不要，我最不需要的就是再買一件 T 恤。

Word
list
1 distinctive [dɪ`stɪŋktɪv] *adj.* 有特色的；獨特的
2 souvenir [`suvəˌnɪr] *n.* .（能使人回憶起旅行、地點、事情的）紀念品、特產
3 rip-off [`rɪpˌɔf] *n.*【俚】索取額外的金錢；敲竹槓；詐騙
4 tacky [`tækɪ] *a.* 俗不可耐的

Part 7

變更計畫

51 延長停留時間

☐ I'd like to extend[1] my stay for two more nights. I can change rooms if necessary.

我想多待兩晚。假如有必要的話，我可以換房間。

☐ I'm not going to check out until Tuesday.

我要到星期二才退房。

☐ My plans have changed. I need my room until the 18th.

我的計畫改變了。我要在我的房間住到十八號為止。

☐ I've been held over.[2] I'll be needing my room for another night.

我延期了。我要在我的房間多住一晚。

☐ Looks like I won't be leaving after all.

看來我暫時還不會離開。

☐ Is it OK if I extend my stay by a day or two?

假如我多待一、兩天，可以嗎？

Word list

1 extand [ɪk`stɛnd] *v.* 把（期限等）延長

2 hold over 將（會議等）延期

52 沒有空房))

☐ Sorry, sir/ma'am. There's nothing available.

抱歉，先生／小姐，沒有空房了。

☐ We're full./We're all booked-up.

我們已經客滿了。／房間都被訂光了。

☐ We're fully booked./The hotel is full.

房間都被訂光了。／飯店客滿了。

☐ I think we can make something work, but you may have to move to a different room.

我想我們可以安排一下，不過你可能必須換個房間。

☐ The only thing we have available is the Presidential Suite.[1]

我們只剩下總統套房了。

☐ I'm sorry, but we just don't have any vacancies.[2] Perhaps you can try the W Hotel.

抱歉，我們沒有任何空房了。也許你可以試試 W 飯店。

Word list
1 presidential suite [ˋprɛzədɛnʃəl ˋswit] *n.* 總統套房
2 vacancy [ˋvekənsɪ] *n.* 空間；（旅館等）空房間

53 更換飯店

☐ Can you recommend a good hotel nearby?

你可以推薦一下附近不錯的飯店嗎？

☐ Where else can I get a room?

我還可以去哪裡找空房？

☐ I'd like something in the same price range.

我想要同等價位的房間。

☐ I don't mind paying more, as long as it's clean. I refuse to stay in filth.[1]

我不介意多付點錢，只要乾淨就好。我可不想住髒的地方。

☐ It would be great if I could get a place near the Convention Center.

假如我能在會議中心附近找到地方住，那就好了。

☐ Do you have anything available for tonight?

你們今天晚上還有空房嗎？

Word list ❶ filth [fɪlθ] *n.* 污穢；骯髒

54 更改班機

電話中

☐ I need to change my flight. My confirmation number is S-K-V-3-5-9. Last name, Lee.
我要換班機。我的確認號碼是 S-K-V-3-5-9，我姓李。

☐ Is there a penalty[1] for changing my flight?
換班機要繳違約金嗎？

☐ I need a later/an earlier flight.
我要晚／早一點的班機。

在機場

☐ I need you to get me on a plane ASAP!
請你幫我安排班機，愈快愈好！

☐ Bumped?[2] What do you mean I've been bumped? Am I waitlisted now?
被擠掉？你說我被擠掉是什麼意思？我現在在候補名單上嗎？

☐ I was told I was confirmed on this flight.
我被告知說，我確定可以搭這班飛機。

Word list
1 penalty [ˋpɛnḷtɪ] *n.* 罰金；罰款
2 bump [bʌmp] *v.* （利用權勢、地位）把……排擠掉；搶走……訂好的座位

55 班機延誤／取消

☐ My flight has been delayed/cancelled.

我的班機延誤／取消了。

☐ All planes have been grounded[1] because of bad weather/a bomb threat.

因為天候不佳／有炸彈威脅，所有的班機都停飛了。

☐ My flight has been pushed back two hours.

我的班機往後延了兩小時。

☐ Apparently there is a problem with the airplane. They said the electrical system.

飛機似乎有問題。他們說是電力系統。

☐ We have to wait while they bring us a new plane/make the repairs.

我們必須等到他們調來新的飛機／修好為止。

☐ The airline ground staff is saying it'll be at least another hour (or two).

航空公司的地勤人員說，起碼還要一（兩）個小時。

Word list **1** ground [graund] v.【航空】使（飛機）不能起飛

56 簽證有問題

☐ This visa is invalid.[1] It's expired.

簽證失效了。它過期了。

☐ Where was your visa issued?[2]

你的簽證是在哪裡發的？

☐ Your visa is good for a single entry only.

你的簽證只能入境一次。

☐ You've overstayed[3] your visa.

你已經超過簽證上的居留時間了。

☐ A tourist visa doesn't allow you to do business while you're in the country.

你不能拿觀光簽證在境內做生意。

☐ Your passport has expired. Please come with me. You're going to be detained.

你的護照過期了。請跟我來。你將遭到拘留。

Word list

1 invalid [ɪn`vælɪd] *adj.*【法律】無效的

2 issue [`ɪʃju] *v.* 發出（命令、佈告、執照等）

3 overstay [`ovɚ`ste] *v.* 比……久留；比……逗留更久

Part **8**

突發狀況

57 生病與買藥

☐ I need to see a doctor. I'm sick/injured.[1]

我要看醫生。我生病 / 受傷了。

☐ Please take me to a medical clinic/hospital.

麻煩帶我去診所 / 醫院。

☐ Can you point me to a pharmacy?[2]

你可以告訴我哪裡有藥局嗎？

☐ I need medicine for a cold/cough/rash[3]/
toothache[4]/earache/stomachache.

我需要治感冒 / 咳嗽 / 疹子 / 牙痛 / 耳朵痛 / 胃痛的藥。

☐ I need something for diarrhea[5]/allergies[6]/
constipation[7]/pain/burns/blisters.[8]

我需要治拉肚子 / 過敏 / 便秘 / 疼痛 / 燙傷 / 水泡的藥。

☐ I'd like this prescription[9] filled, please.

我想要配這帖處方的藥，麻煩你。

Word list

1 injured [`ɪndʒəd] *adj.* 受傷的；負傷的
2 pharmacy [`farməsɪ] *n.* 藥局
3 rash [ræʃ] *n.*【醫學】發疹；皮疹
4 ache [ek] *n.* 疼痛酸痛（常構成複合字，如
toothache 牙痛，stomachache 胃痛）
5 diarrhea [ˌdaɪə`riə] *n.*【醫學】腹瀉

6 allergy [`ælədʒɪ] *n.* 過敏症
7 constipation [ˌkɑnstə`peʃən] *n.*【醫學】
便秘
8 blister [`blɪstə] *n.* （皮膚的）水泡
9 prescription [prɪ`skrɪpʃən] *n.* 處方；藥方

58 受傷與就醫

CD1 60

☐ I'm in a lot of pain. It hurts here.

我痛得不得了。這裡很痛。

☐ I'm allergic[1] to cats/peanuts/penicillin.[2]

我對貓／花生／盤尼西林過敏。

☐ I feel dizzy/feverish[3]/nauseous[4]/sore.

我覺得頭暈／發燒／噁心／痛。

☐ I sprained[5] my ankle./I cut my finger.

我的腳踝扭傷了。／我的手指割傷了。

☐ Please call an ambulance. I'm having a heart/asthmatic[6]/panic attack.

麻煩去叫救護車。我的心臟病／氣喘／恐慌症犯了。

☐ I'm having trouble breathing/sleeping/walking/hearing/eating/urinating.[7]

我沒辦法呼吸／睡覺／走路／聽到／吃東西／排尿。

Word list

1 allergic [ə`lɝdʒɪk] *adj.* 過敏（性）的；對……過敏的（~ to sth.）

2 penicillin [ˌpɛnɪ`sɪlɪn] *n.* 盤尼西林；青黴素

3 feverish [`fivərɪʃ] *adj.* 發燒的

4 nauseous [`nɔʃəs] *adj.*【美口語】反胃的；想嘔的

5 sprain [spren] *v.* 扭傷（腳踝等）

6 asthmatic [æz`mætɪk] *adj.* 氣喘的／ *n.* 氣喘患者

7 urinate [`jurəˌnet] *v.* 排尿；小便

59 通報意外

☐ There's been an accident. Send help.

有意外發生。快找人來幫忙。

☐ There are injuries.[1] Call the paramedics.[2]

有人受傷了。找醫療人員來。

☐ Please send the police/the fire department/
an ambulance/a doctor/a rescue team.

請派警察／消防隊／救護車／醫生／救援小組來。

☐ There's smoke in the hallway. Fire!

大廳有煙。失火了！

☐ You need to sound the fire alarm.

你得去通報火警。

☐ There is a person/are people trapped in the elevator. Call for
help. Call 911.[3]

有人被困在電梯裡。找人來幫忙，打九一一。

Word
list
  1 injury [`ɪndʒərɪ] *n.* （意外事件引起的）傷害；損傷

  2 paramedic [͵pærə`mɛdɪk] *n.* 護理人員；醫療輔助人員

  3 911　美國緊急通報電話（相當於台灣的 119 通報專線）

60 通報失竊

☐ I've lost my room key.

我的房間鑰匙搞丟了。

☐ My wallet is missing.

我的錢包不見了。

☐ I seem to have misplaced[1] my passport.

我好像把護照忘在什麼地方了。

☐ I can't find my cellular phone anywhere.

我到處都找不到我的手機。

☐ Do you have a lost-and-found?[2]

你們有失物招領處嗎？

☐ Has anyone turned in[3] a digital camera?

有人撿到數位相機嗎？

Word
list
1 misplace [mɪs`ples] *v.* 遺忘；擱忘
2 lost-and-found [`lost ˌɛnd `faʊnd] *n.* 失物招領處
3 turn in 將……交與警方

61 通報重罪

☐ I was mugged¹/raped/assaulted²/robbed.

我遭到了襲擊 / 強暴 / 攻擊 / 搶劫。

☐ I was raped. I was sexually assaulted.

我被強暴了。我受到了性侵害。

☐ A man/woman attacked me (with a knife).

有個男的 / 女的（拿刀）攻擊我。

☐ Someone is following/harassing³ me.

有人跟蹤 / 騷擾我。

☐ I'd like to report a theft.

我想通報失竊。

☐ Someone stole my wallet from my hotel room. I left at six. When I returned at nine, it was gone. The door was locked.

有人到我的飯店房間裡偷了我的皮夾。我在六點離開。等我在九點回去時，它就不見了，而且門是鎖著的。

Word
list
1 mug [mʌg] v. （強盜、刺客等）從背後襲擊

2 assault [əˋsɔlt] v. 突襲；攻擊

3 harass [həˋræs] v. 使……煩擾；折磨（人）

62 避免被敲竹槓／被騙 CD1 64

☐ It's too much. I'll give you half, OK?

太貴了。我給你一半好嗎？

☐ The quality is a little suspect.[1] Look, there's something wrong here. [point to defect[2]]

品質有點可疑。你看，這裡有問題。（指出缺點）

☐ It's obviously a cheap knock-off.[3] Thirty bucks ($30.00) is as high as I'll go.

這顯然是個廉價的仿冒品。我頂多出到三十塊。

☐ This is clearly a pirated[4] version.

這顯然是盜版。

☐ It's not real. Look at that fake logo!

這不是真品。你看這個假商標！

☐ I've been had![5] I bought a bogus[6] bag!

我被騙了！我買到了假的包包！

Word list

1 suspect [sə`spɛkt] *adj.* 令人懷疑的；可疑的

2 defect [dɪ`fɛkt] *n.* 缺點；瑕疵

3 knock-off [`nɑk͵ɔf] *n.* 冒牌服裝；售價低廉的仿造品（= knockoff）

4 pirated [`paɪrətɪd] *adj.* 盜印的；未經允許擅自出版的

5 have [hæv]【英口語】詐欺；欺騙

6 bogus [`bogəs] *adj.* 假的；偽造的

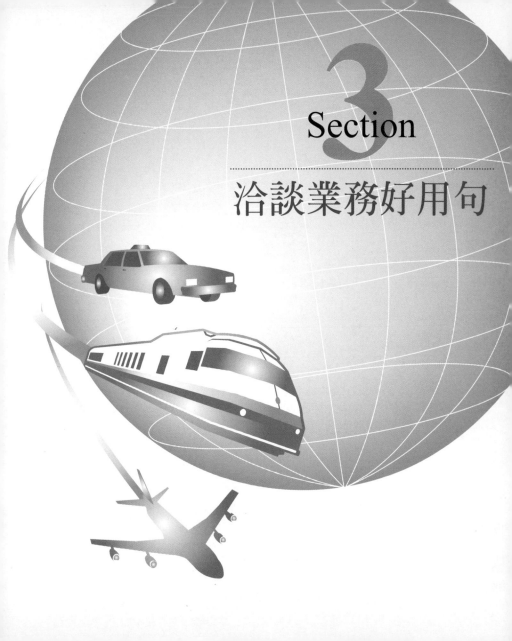

Section 3

洽談業務好用句

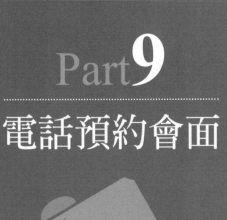

Part 9

電話預約會面

約時間

☐ When can we meet to talk this over?

我們什麼時候可以見面好好談談這件事？

☐ When would be a good time for us to meet?

我們什麼時候見面比較好？

☐ Do you have time to meet tomorrow around 9 a.m.?

你明天九點左右有時間見個面嗎？

☐ We need to schedule[1] a meeting. When are you free?

我們得約個時間見面。你什麼時候有空？

☐ What's your schedule like over the next few days?

你接下來幾天有時間嗎？

☐ When's best for you?

你覺得什麼時間最好？

Word list　**1** schedule [`skɛdʒʊl] *v.* 將……排入時間表中；預定，安排

64　確認會面

☐ I just want to confirm we're still on[1] for tomorrow.

　我只是想確認一下，我們明天還是照約。

☐ We're supposed to meet at three-thirty tomorrow. Does that still work for you?

　我們明天應該要在三點半見面。你還是可以赴約嗎？

☐ Are we still on for Wednesday at four (o'clock)?

　我們還是照樣約星期三的四點嗎？

☐ I just wanted to double check — our meeting is at ten (o'clock), right?

　我只是想再確認一次，我們十點見面對吧？

☐ Our meeting is scheduled for 9 a.m. Is that OK?

　我們約了早上九點見面。沒問題吧？

☐ So I'll see you at the meeting at three (o'clock).

　那我三點的時候可以在會議上看到你。

Part 9 電話預約會面

Word list　**1** on [ɑn] *adj.* 有計畫的；預期的

65 重訂見面時間

CD2 03

在說這些話之前，不妨先說句：I'm sorry, but...「我很抱歉……」

☐ I'm afraid I can't make our meeting.

恐怕我沒辦法赴約了。

☐ Something urgent has come up, and I'm going to have to reschedule.

有急事發生，所以我非得重訂時間不可。

☐ I've got a scheduling conflict.[1] Can we make it another time?

我的時間撞期了。我們可以改約別的時間嗎？

☐ I've been called away,[2] so I won't be available until next week/next month.

我接到了任務，所以要到下星期／下個月才有空。

☐ Can we move our meeting up/back to Friday instead?

我們可以把見面的時間提前／挪後到星期五嗎？

☐ Mike Dunlop's got to go to Singapore next Wednesday. Is it possible for us to meet before then?

麥克‧鄧洛普下星期三必須跑一趟新加坡，我們可以趕在之前見個面嗎？

Word list

[1] conflict [`kɑnflɪkt] n. 衝突

[2] call away （從座位上）把……叫走；叫……離座退席（常用被動語態）

66 更改見面地點

如果適當的話，在說以面這些話前，你可以先說：I've just found out...「我剛發現……」
或 I've just been told...「我剛得知……」

☐ We need a bigger room. We're going to move the meeting to the Nangang office, OK?

我們需要更大的房間。我們改在南港辦公室見面好嗎？

☐ The boardroom[1] is booked for that time. I need to find us a new location.

會議室那個時段有人訂了。我得找個新地點才行。

☐ We're renovating[2] the eleventh floor and there are contractors[3] everywhere. Can we meet at your office instead?

我們在整修十一樓，所以到處都是工人。我們可以改到你們的辦公室見面嗎？

☐ I can't get us a lunch reservation at Grosvenor's–they're fully booked.

我在格洛斯沃訂不到午餐的位子，他們位子都訂滿了。

☐ We need to find a new place to meet.

我們得換個地方見面。

☐ How about we meet at the Mayfair Club instead? Same time.

我們改到美菲俱樂部見面怎麼樣？時間不變。

Word list
1 boardroom [`bord,rum] *n.* 會議室；董事會會議室
2 renovate [`rɛnə,vet] *v.* 使……變新；修理；修繕
3 contractor [`kɑntræktə] *n.* 立契約者；承包者；承攬人

Part 9 電話預約會面

67 換人赴約

☐ Kelly Jones can't make the meeting, but we're going to go ahead without her.

凱利·瓊斯沒辦法來開會，但我們的約定照舊。

☐ I can't be there myself, so Michael Timmins is going to stand in[1] for me.

我沒辦法親自出席，所以麥可·提明斯會代表我去。

☐ Al Collins is going to take my place.[2]

艾爾·柯林斯會代替我去。

☐ There's no point having the meeting if John Godfrey can't attend.

假如約翰·加弗瑞不能出席，那開會就沒意義了。

☐ Ross Bell can't make it in person, but we'll set up a conference call[3]/video conference.[4]

羅斯·貝爾沒辦法親自出席，可是我們會辦一場電話／視訊會議。

☐ Allan Reeves is going to be a no-show.

艾倫·李夫斯無法依約出席。

Word list
1 stand in 代理、代替（某人）
2 take one's place 代理、代替（某人）
3 conference call [`kɑnfərəns ˌkɔl] n. 電話會議
4 video conference [`vɪdɪˌo ˌkɑnfərəns] n. 視訊會議
5 no-show [`noˌʃo] n.【口語】預訂座位卻未出席的人；不能依約出席的人

68 詢問細節

CD2 06

有多少人要參加，以及事先要準備哪些資料和器材最好先問清楚。

☐ So how many people are you bringing in total?
那你們總共會有多少人？

☐ So it will just be the three of us, then?
那到時候只會有我們三個人？

☐ Do you need anything special set up in advance for your presentation?
你的報告需要什麼特別的事前作業嗎？

☐ What kind of A/V (audio-visual) equipment¹ do you need?
你需要哪種視聽設備？

☐ Will you be using Powerpoint?
你會用到 Powerpoint 嗎？

☐ How many copies (of the material) should I make?
我應該準備多少份（資料）？

Part
9
電
話
預
約
會
面

Word list ❶ audio-visual equipment [ˈɔdɪo ˈvɪʒʊəl ɪˈkwɪpmənt] *n.* 視聽設備
(= A/V equipment)

Part 10

參加商展

69 如何前往展場

詢問從飯店抵達展場的相關問題。

☐ Can you give me directions to the venue?[1]

你能告訴我會場怎麼走嗎？

☐ The map/directions you sent out isn't/aren't exactly clear.

你寄來的地圖／指示不是很清楚。

☐ We'll be coming in from the north/south/east/west.

我們會從北／南／東／西邊進去。

☐ What's the closest major intersection?

最靠近的主要交流道是哪一個？

☐ Could you give me the street address again, please?

可以麻煩你再把地址給我一次嗎？

☐ I assume it will be easy to recognize the venue/hotel/convention center.

我想那個地點／飯店／會議中心不會很難認。

Word list **1** venue [`vɛnju] *n.* 集會場所；會場；舉辦地點

70 向主辦單位報到

☐ Hi, we're with Fester Medical. Can you show us where we'll be setting up?

嗨，我們是 Fester Medical。你可以告訴我們預定的攤位在哪裡嗎？

☐ Hello, I'm with Guantex. Where do I go to register?

你好，我是 Guantex。我要去哪裡登記？

☐ Here are our registration documents.

這是我們的登記文件。

☐ We've been assigned booth number twenty-seven. Where is that?

我們分配到的攤位是二十七號。它在什麼地方？

☐ Is there anything else we need to do before we start setting up?

開始架設前，我們還需要做些什麼嗎？

☐ Is there an area where we can pull up[1] the van[2] to unload[3]/load it?

有地方可以讓我們停車卸／裝貨嗎？

Word list
1 pull up 把（馬或車子）停下來
2 van [væn] *n.* 小型有蓋貨車
3 unload [ʌn`lod] *v.* 從……卸貨；卸下（載貨）（← load [lod] *v.* 將貨物裝於……）

71 解決問題 1

☐ I'm a little concerned with the visibility[1] of our booth.

我有點擔心我們攤位不夠醒目。

☐ That signboard[2] is blocking access to our booth. Can it be moved?

這個布告欄擋住了我們攤位的視線。可以把它移開嗎？

☐ The space you've assigned us doesn't fit the description you gave over the phone.

你們分配給我們的地點跟你們在電話中描述的不一樣。

☐ We require two additional tables/chairs.

我們還需要兩張桌子／椅子。

☐ I'm sorry, but this is unacceptable.

抱歉，這實在讓人無法接受。

☐ We need access to electrical outlets.[3]

我們需要用電源插座。

Word list

1 visibility [ˌvɪzə`bɪlətɪ] *n.* 可見性；明顯性；能見度

2 signboard [`saɪnˌbord] *n.* 招牌

3 outlet [`autˌlɛt] *n.*【美】（電的）插座

72 解決問題 2

當你和隔壁的攤位有爭議需要請人幫忙解決時，就可以對主辦單位這麼說。

☐ We're having some problems with the booth next door.
我們跟隔壁的攤位有點爭議。

☐ The music from that booth is drowning out our video/presentation/salespeople.
那個攤位的音樂蓋掉了我們影片／報告／推銷員的聲音。

☐ They're encroaching[1] on our space.
他們占用了我們的空間。

☐ We've spoken to them about it, but the situation hasn't changed.
我們跟他們說過了，可是情況並沒有改善。

☐ We'd appreciate it if you could have a word with them.[2]
假如你們能跟他們溝通一下，我們會很感激。

☐ Maybe it would be better if you spoke to them (about the problem).
假如你們去跟他們講一下（這個問題），也許會比較好。

Word list
1 encroach [ɪnˋkrotʃ] v. 侵入（他人、他國的土地等）；侵害（他人的權利等）
2 have a word with 對……說（尤其是私下的或秘密的事）

73 向客人自我介紹

☐ Please allow me to introduce myself. My name is...
我來自我介紹，我叫做……。

☐ I'm Pei-Chen Wu, Director of Sales and Marketing at ChangeRite.
我叫吳培辰，是 ChangeRite 的業務及行銷主任。

☐ My name is Mark Gamble and I represent Silton Fiber-optics.[1]
我叫做馬克・甘博，代表 Silton 光纖。

☐ I'm very pleased to meet you. My name is Vincent Chen.
很高興認識你。我叫做文森・陳。

☐ I'm with Variloc Security Systems.
我是 Variloc 保全系統。

☐ Vincent Chen, Sell-Well Pharmaceuticals.[2] How do you do?
文森・陳，Sell-Well 藥廠，您好。

Word list
1 fiber-optic [ˋfaɪbɚˋɑptɪks] *n.* 光纖
2 pharmaceuticals [ˏfɑrməˋsutɪkḷ] *n.* 藥物 / *adj.* 製藥的

74 介紹他人

☐ I'd like to introduce Tony Champagne.
我來介紹湯尼・陳賓。

☐ Tony's part of our team here at the trade fair[1]/trade show.
湯尼是我們在這次展銷會／商展中的團隊成員。

☐ Tony's in charge of[2] product placement for the company.
湯尼負責公司的置入行銷。

☐ Tony's/Toni's the man/woman to speak to about product placement.
湯尼是置入行銷的聯絡人。

☐ Tony looks after[3] product placement for Iron-on Corp.
湯尼負責 Iron-on 公司的置入行銷。

☐ Tony heads up[4] the product placement department/team at Iron-on Corp.
湯尼是 Iron-on 公司置入行銷部門／團隊的負責人。

Word list

1 fair [fɛr] *n.* 博覽會；樣品展示會
2 in charge of 照顧（管理、擔任）……的
3 look after 照料……；小心看管……
4 head up 領導；統籌

75 簡便推銷用語

試著用下面的句子宣傳新產品，吸引潛在的合作伙伴。

☐ We've got some great new products.

我們有一些很棒的新產品。

☐ We're really excited about our new line of desktop organizers.[1]

我們新款的桌上行事曆使我們倍感興奮。

☐ We've got some new products that are guaranteed[2] to blow your mind.[3]

我們有一些很棒的新產品，保證讓你動心。

☐ Our flat-screen monitors are state-of-the-art.[4]

我們的平面顯示器很先進。

☐ The technology this product represents is on the cutting edge[5] of the industry.

這個產品採用的是業界頂尖的技術。

☐ We're re-defining the industry with these interfaces.[6]

我們以這些介面重新定義了這個產業。

Word List

1 organizer [ˈɔrgəˌnaɪzɚ] *n.* 萬用記事本

2 guarantee [ˌgærənˈti] *v.* 保證（商品等）

3 blow one's mind 令人感覺十分興奮；令人驚訝

4 state-of-the-art [ˈstetəvði ˈɑrt] *adj.* （科技、機電等產品）最先進的；最高級的

5 cutting edge [ˈkʌtɪŋ ˈɛdʒ] *n.* 最前線；尖端

6 interface [ˈɪntɚˌfes] *n.* 介面；交界點；切點

76 談論產品

☐ Our gem[1] polisher meets all your requirements, and more.
我們的寶石磨光機符合你們的一切要求，而且更好。

☐ GemWash is the perfect solution to your problem.
GemWash 最能解決你們的問題。

☐ GemWash is the answer to your prayers.[2]
GemWash 正符合你們的期待。

☐ That's exactly the kind of problem GemWash was designed to eliminate.[3]
這就是 GemWash 專門要解決的那種問題。

☐ We can tailor-make[4] our gem polishers to suit your require-ments.
我們可以特別設計寶石磨光機，以符合你們的要求。

☐ We can customize[5] our gem polishers to suit your needs.[6]
我們可以訂做寶石磨光機，以符合你們的需求。

Word list

1 gem [dʒɛm] *n.* （由指經過琢磨之）寶石；珠寶

2 prayer [prɛɚ] *n.* 請願；請求之事

3 eliminate [ɪˋlɪməˌnet] *v.* 剔除；除去

4 tailor-make [ˋtelɚˋmek] *v.* 特製；專門設計

5 customize [ˋkʌstəmˌaɪz] *v.* 訂做；客製

6 suit one's need　符合……的需求

下面這些句子可誘使客人待久一點。

☐ I'd love to sit down with you and talk about our products.

我想跟你坐下來談談我們的產品。

☐ If you're interested, I think we should sit down and I can go into some more detail about what we can offer.

假如你有興趣的話,我想我們應該坐下來,我會更詳細地介紹我們所能提供的東西。

☐ Why don't you have a seat, and I can show you some samples?

你何不坐下來,好讓我給你看一些樣品?

☐ Why don't you take a look at some of our brochures[1]/promotional[2] materials?

你何不看看我們的一些文宣/促銷內容?

☐ Let me show you something.

讓我來跟你介紹一下。

☐ Take a look at this.

你看這個。

Word list
1 brochure [bro`ʃur] *n.* 小冊子
2 promotional [prə`moʃənl] *adj.* 促銷的

78 送客人樣品

你可能會聽到

☐ Do you have any samples?
你們有什麼樣品嗎？

你可以說

☐ Please, take one, with our compliments.[1]
請拿一份我們的贈品。

☐ Help yourself.
請自取。

☐ Please accept a small gift (from us).
請笑納一份（我們送的）小禮物。

☐ Here's a complimentary[2] travel pillow/pen set.
這是贈送的旅行枕／筆組。

☐ Here's a sample for you.
這是送你的樣品。

Word list
1 compliment [ˋkɑmpləmənt] *n.* 讚美的話；恭維；敬意
2 complimentary [ˌkɑmpləˋmɛntərɪ] *adj.* 免費的；贈送的

79 交換聯絡方式 1

給對方電話號碼或名片。

☐ Take my card.

收下我的名片。

☐ Here's my card.

這是我的名片。

☐ Please take my card. All my contact info is on there.

請收下我的名片。我的聯絡方式全部在上面。

☐ I'm easy to reach.[1] Call my mobile/cell/office phone any time.

我很好找。隨時可以打我的手機／大哥大／辦公室電話。

☐ I'll be waiting to hear from you.[2]

我會等你的消息。

☐ If there's anything I can do for you, don't hesitate to call.

假如有什麼我可以效勞的地方，儘管打電話來。

Word List

1 reach [ritʃ] v.（以電話等）聯絡

2 hear from sb. 收到……的信（或電報）

80 交換聯絡方式 2

CD2 18

索取對方的電話號碼或名片。

☐ Do you have a card?
你有名片嗎？

☐ When's the best time to reach you?
什麼時間找你最好？

☐ What's the best way to contact you?
怎麼聯絡你最好？

☐ What's your mobile/cell/office phone number?
你的手機／大哥大／辦公室電話號碼是多少？

☐ Is there an extension?[1]
有分機嗎？

☐ I'll be in touch.[2]
我會保持聯絡。

Word list
[1] extension [ɪk`stɛnʃən] n. （電話的）分機；內線
[2] in touch (with) （與人）保持聯絡

81 敲定買賣 1

你拿到生意了！

☐ Which product are you interested in?

你對哪樣產品有興趣？

☐ So how many pieces/units are we talking about?

那我們談的是多少件／套？

☐ So how many pieces/units do you need?

那你需要多少件／套？

☐ Why don't we write up the order right now?

我們何不馬上詳細列出訂單？

☐ I'll put you down[1] for a quantity of ten thousand units.

我會幫你一萬套的數量寫下來。

☐ We'll send that shipment[2] out right away.

我們會立刻把那批貨送過去。

Word list
1 put down　寫下⋯⋯的名字
2 shipment [ˈʃɪpmənt] *n.* 運貨；發貨

82 敲定買賣 2

CD2 20

和客人談及書面手續和付款條件可用下列句子。

☐ I need you to sign here, please.
請你在這邊簽名。

☐ I need your signature[1] right here, please.
麻煩你把名字簽在這裡。

☐ We'll need your chop[2] to complete the transaction.
我們需要你們蓋個章,交易才算完成。

☐ How will you be paying?
你們要怎麼付款?

☐ All sales are final.
所有的買賣都確定了。

☐ We take cash, credit card, or certified check.[3] No personal checks, sorry!
我們接受現金、信用卡或保付支票。個人支票不行,抱歉!

Part *10* 參加商展

Word list

1 signature [`sɪgnətʃɚ] *n.* 簽名

2 chop [tʃɑp] *n.* (印度、中國的)官印;公章;圖章

3 certified check [`sɝtəfaɪd `tʃɛk] *n.* (銀行)保付支票

83 買賣條件

保證、保固、更換和退貨規定的相關說法。

☐ We stand behind our products one hundred percent.

我們對本公司的產品百分之百負責。

☐ All our products are guaranteed[1] against defects[2] in materials and workmanship for a period of one year.

我們所有的產品都享有一年的材料與製作瑕疵擔保。

☐ Satisfaction is guaranteed, or we'll gladly refund[3] your money.

保證滿意，否則我們很樂意退錢。

☐ The warranty[4] period is two years.

保固期是兩年。

☐ The warranty covers parts[5] and labor.

保固包含零件和人工。

☐ Our policy is to allow exchanges within thirty days, but we don't offer refunds.

我們的規定是三十天內可以更換，可是不接受退費。

Word list

1 guarante [`gærən`ti] v. 保證（商品等）

2 defect [dɪ`fɛkt] n. 缺陷；缺點；瑕疵

3 refund [rɪ`fʌnd] v. 退還

4 warranty [`wɔrəntɪ] n.（商品、品質等的）保證（書）

5 part [pɑrt] n.（機器；器具的）零件

84 運送／交付協議

☐ We can ship that to you immediately.
我們可以立刻把它寄運過去。

☐ We'll get that order out to you first thing on Friday.
我們在星期五一早就會把那批貨送去給你。

☐ We guarantee delivery within ten days of receiving an order.
我們保證在收到訂單的十天內送到。

☐ We have a thirty-day turnaround[1] period on orders.
我們有三十天的期限完成訂單。

☐ We can send that to you by bonded[2] courier.[3]
我們可以用擔保快遞把它送過去。

☐ We have our own fleet[4] of delivery vehicles.
我們有自己的送貨車隊。

Word list

1 turnaround [`tɝnə͵raund] *n.* 一件工作自接下到完成所需的時間

2 bonded [`bɑndɪd] *adj.* 附有擔保的

3 courier [`kʊrɪɚ] *n.* 急件（快函）的遞送人

4 fleet [flit] *n.* （同一家公司所有的）全部車輛

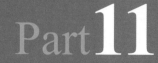

Part 11

出席研討會／
產業智庫

85 表達對主題／講者的興趣 CD2 23

可用下列句子表達你對講者及講題的興趣。

☐ I'm very excited to hear Dr. Gambol's talk.
我很興奮能聽到甘博博士講話。

☐ This will be a great opportunity to exchange ideas.
這會是個交換意見的大好機會。

☐ I'm looking forward to discussing Dr. Gambol's findings/research/work (with him/her).
我很期待能（和他／她）討論甘博的發現／研究／作品。

☐ I'm looking forward to picking Dr. Gambol's brain.[1]
我很期待能向甘博請益。

☐ I thought Dr. Gambol had some fascinating ideas about alternative[2] therapies.[3]
我覺得甘博博士對另類療法有一些很棒的想法。

☐ It's a real treat[4] to have the opportunity to meet Dr. Gambol.
有機會見到甘博博士真的很難得。

Word list

1 pick one's brain 向……請益

2 alternative [ɔl`tɜnətɪv] *adj.* 另類的；非傳統的；非主流的

3 therapy [`θɛrəpɪ] *n.* 療法

4 treat [trit] *n.* （少有的）快樂的、喜悅

86 開場

用下列句子介紹你將要談論的內容。

☐ I've prepared some notes that I'll be reading from.
我準備了一些要報告的重點。

☐ I hope I'm prepared... there'll be a lot of questions, I'm sure.
希望我準備得夠充分……我相信大家會有很多問題。

☐ It's a privilege[1] to get to speak to such a distinguished[2] group of entrepreneurs[3]/managers/professionals.
很榮幸能對一群這麼傑出的企業家／經理人／專業人士講點話。

☐ I'm honored to have the chance to give a speech/make a presentation.
很榮幸有這個機會發言／報告。

☐ I hope that our research/findings can help the whole industry/medical community.
希望我們的研究／發現能對整個產業／醫界有幫助。

☐ No matter how many times I do it, I always get nervous before making a presentation/speech.
無論有多少次經驗，我在報告／發言前總是會緊張。

Word list

1 privilege [ˈprɪvlɪdʒ] *n.* 殊榮；特權
2 distinguished [dɪˈstɪŋgwɪʃt] *adj.* 超群的；卓越的
3 entrepreneur [ˌɑntrəprəˈnɝ] *n.* 企業家

87 介紹發言人／講者 🔊

☐ John, welcome to Chicago.

約翰，歡迎來芝加哥。

☐ Ladies and gentlemen, we'll be on the eleventh floor. Please follow me.

各位，我們會在十一樓。請跟我來。

☐ Welcome, distinguished guests.

歡迎各位貴賓。

☐ Dr. Gambol will be the keynote[1] speaker.

甘博博士將擔任主講人。

☐ You're all probably familiar with Dr. Gambol's work/research (by now).

各位大概都很熟悉甘博博士（到目前為止）的作品／研究。

☐ Ron Gambol has become a household[2] name.

隆恩・甘博已經成為家喻戶曉的名人。

Word list
1 keynote [ˋkiˏnot] *n.* （演說的）主旨
2 household [ˋhausˏhold] *adj.* 家喻戶曉的；為人熟知的（~ name 名人）

88 說明時間表和用餐情形 🔊 CD2 26

☐ We start at 8:30 a.m. with a presentation by Ray Iverson.

我們從早上八點半由雷‧艾佛森開始報告。

☐ Breakfast will be served (starting at) 7:00 a.m.

早餐將在早上七點（開始）供應。

☐ We'll be stopping for a break at 10:30.

十點半會中場休息。

☐ There will be coffee and donuts at the break.

休息時會有咖啡和甜甜圈。

☐ We'll break[1] for lunch from noon to one o'clock.

午餐時間從正午到一點。

☐ We'll get started again at one o'clock.

下半場從一點開始。

Word list **1** break [brek] *v./n.* 休息；停止工作

Part 12

參觀工廠

89 表達興趣

☐ It will be good to have a look at your operation.
能去你們那邊看看你們的作業也好。

☐ I've been looking forward to this tour for a long time.
我對這次的參訪已經期待很久了。

☐ I'm keen to have a look around.
我很想到處看看。

☐ So this is where it all happens!
一切都是在這裡搞出來的！

☐ I'm especially interested in seeing the wind tunnel.
我對於參觀風洞特別感興趣。

☐ It's very similar to our factory/lab[1] in Holland.
它跟我們在荷蘭的工廠／實驗室很像。

Word list　**1** lab [læb] *n.* 實驗室；研究室（= laboratory 的縮寫）

90 表達滿意

☐ Very impressive![1]

真了不起！

☐ I'm impressed with the efficiency of your production lines.

你們生產線的效率讓我印象深刻。

☐ I'm more than satisfied with the cleanliness of the storage[2] area.

我對於存放區的清潔相當滿意。

☐ It's immaculate![3]

真是一點瑕疵都沒有！

☐ You run a tight ship[4] here!

你們把這裡經營得真好！

☐ It's an impressive operation/facility.

真是了不起的營運／地方。

Word list

1 impressive [ɪmˋprɛsɪv] *adj.* 令人印象深刻

2 storage [ˋstorɪdʒ] *n.* 倉庫（保管）

3 immaculate [ɪˋmækjəlɪt] *adj.* 無污點的；沒有缺點的

4 run a tight ship 把（事業、家庭等）經營、管理得很好

91 表達不滿 1

☐ I must say I'm not overly impressed with the overall cleanliness of the operation.

我必須說，我對於整個廠區清潔的印象不是很好。

☐ The place is a mess!

這裡真是亂！

☐ There are safety hazards[1] all over the place.

這裡到處都有工安危機。

☐ There are some major hygiene[2] issues/fire hazards here!

這裡有一些重大的衛生問題／火災危機！

☐ This will have to be sorted out[3]/cleaned up before we can do business.

這必須先經過整頓／整理，我們才能做生意。

☐ This, for example, is an accident waiting to happen.

比方說，這就是可能發生的意外。

Word list

1 hazard [`hæzɚd] *n.* 危險；風險

2 hygiene [`haɪdʒin] *n.* 衛生；衛生學

3 sort out 【英口語】整理、整頓；解決（問題、糾紛等）

92 表達不滿 2

☐ Are you sure you'll be able to handle the quantities we talked about?

你確定你們能應付我們所談的數量嗎？

☐ The workers don't look very busy/happy.

工人看起來不怎麼忙／開心。

☐ How much did you say you pay your workers?

你說你們給工人的薪水是多少？

☐ This is a sweatshop.[1]

這是間壓榨人的工廠。

☐ I wasn't aware you used child labor. This is a big problem for us.

我不知道你們雇用童工。我們認為這是個很大的問題。

☐ These working/sanitary[2] conditions are appalling.[3]

這些工作／衛生條件很糟糕。

Word list

1 sweatshop [ˋswɛt͵ʃɑp] *n.* 壓榨勞力的工廠

2 sanitary [ˋsænə͵tɛrɪ] *adj.* 衛生的；保健方面的

3 appalling [əˋpɔlɪŋ] *adj.* 【口語】過分的；不像話的；很糟的

Part **13**

....

做簡報

93 見面與問候

最後一句只適用於早上。

☐ Ladies and gentlemen, good morning/afternoon/evening.
各位早安／午安／晚安。

☐ It's a pleasure for me to be here today.
很高興今天能來到這裡。

☐ You'll see in front of you a handout[1] I've prepared. I'll be referring to it often.
各位在面前會看到我所準備的提綱。我會經常提到它。

☐ I don't intend to keep you long this morning/afternoon/evening.
今天早上／下午／晚上我不打算耽誤各位太久的時間。

☐ It's nice to see so many smiling faces!
看到這麼多笑臉真好！

☐ Everyone looks bright-eyed and bushy-tailed![2]
大家看起來都充滿了朝氣！

Word list

1 handout [`hændaʊt] *n.* 講義；廣告傳單

2 bright-eyed and bushy-tailed 朝氣蓬勃的；充滿朝氣的

94 自我介紹

CD2 32

用這些話為你的發言開場。

☐ For those of you who don't know me, my name is Denise Chen.
如果有人不認識我的話，我叫做丹妮絲・陳。

☐ I am the Junior/Senior Vice-president of Prudhomme Insurance in charge of the Legal Department.
我是 Prudhomme 保險的副總裁／資深副總裁，主管法務部門。

☐ I have worked for Prudhomme Insurance for most of the last twenty years.
過去二十年來，我都是在 Prudhomme 保險服務。

☐ I should say before we start that it's my pleasure to have been invited to speak to you today.
在開始前，我想說的是，很高興今天受邀來跟各位報告。

☐ I'd like to preface[1] my remarks[2] by saying how happy I am to be able to give this presentation.
在發言的一開始，我想說的是，很高興能負責這次的報告。

☐ I'd like to start off by mentioning my gratitude to my assistant, Roberta Black, for all her help in preparing the data for today's presentation.
一開始我想先向我的助理蘿貝塔・布萊克致意，以感謝她全力協助我準備今天報告的資料。

Word list
1 preface [ˋprɛfɪs] *v.* 作為⋯的開端
2 remark [rɪˋmɑrk] *n.* 意見評論話語 (=comment)

95 以數據／資料／統計數字來說明 CD2 33

每個人都在聽，你能用數字說出什麼道理？

☐ I'll draw your attention to page two of the handout.
請各位注意提綱的第二頁。

☐ If you'll look up here, I've prepared a graph[1]/graphic[2] to show sales figures over the last quarter/past three years.
假如各位看這裡的話，我準備了圖表來說明上一季／過去三年的銷售數字。

☐ The numbers don't lie.
數字不會騙人。

☐ The numbers bear out[3] that production has fallen off sharply/increased steadily over the last quarter/past three years.
數字證明，上一季／過去三年的產量急速下跌／持續增加。

☐ The numbers confirm our worst fears.
數字證實了我們最擔心的事。

☐ What we predicted[4] has/has not come to pass.
我們預測的事成真了／沒有成真。

Word list

1 graph [græf] *n.* 曲線圖；圖表；圖解

2 graphic [`græfɪk] *n.* 藝術平面作品

3 bear out 證實；支持（所說的話、理論等）

4 predict [prɪ`dɪkt] *v.* 預言……；預測……

96 討論目標

 CD2 34

清楚說明公司所要走的方向。

☐ Our main priority is/has been/was to improve employee satisfaction and productivity.

我們的首要之務是改善員工滿意度及生產力。

☐ Our aim is/has been/was to improve efficiency as well as after-sales services.

我們的目標是要改善效率與售後服務。

☐ The short-/medium-/long-term goal is to maintain control of our major markets.

短期／中期／長期目標是要持續掌控我們的主要市場。

☐ We've changed our strategy to meet market conditions.

我們調整了策略，以因應市場狀況。

☐ Our new orientation[1] reflects the fact that we've been forced to downsize.[2]

我們的新取向反映了我們被迫縮編的事實。

☐ We're determined to turn this thing around.

我們決心要扭轉這種局面。

Word list
1 orientation [ˌorɪɛnˋteʃən] 定位；方針（或態度的）確認
2 downsize [ˋdaʊnˋsaɪz] v. 縮編；裁減（員工）人數

☐ We've been conducting[1] research on stem-cell[2] technology.

我們一直在研究幹細胞的技術。

☐ Our field of study is genome[3] mapping.

我們的研究領域是描繪基因圖譜。

☐ Our research has shed light on factors predisposing[4] patients to depression.[5]

我們的研究著重在導致病患憂鬱的因素上。

☐ Our research has resulted in a major breakthrough in prosthetic[6] capabilities.[7]

我們的研究在義肢功能方面獲得了重大突破。

☐ Our research has had some startling[8]/unexpected results.

我們的研究得到了一些驚人／意料之外的結果。

☐ Our research has shown that the robotic soldier is a real possibility.

我們的研究顯示，機器士兵真的有可能。

Word list

1. conduct [kən`dʌkt] v. 經營；管理
2. stem-cell [`stɛm,sɛl] n. 幹細胞
3. genome [`dʒi,nom] n. 基因組
4. predispose [,pridɪs`poz]【醫學】使（人）易患（疾病）
5. depression [dɪ`prɛʃən] n. 意志消沈；憂鬱；沮喪
6. prosthetic [prɑs`θɛtɪk] adj.【醫學】義肢的；假體的
7. capability [,kepə`bɪlətɪ] n.（東西所具有的）特性；性能
8. startling [`stɑrtlɪŋ] adj. 使人吃驚的；驚人的

98

排除干擾

有人搞不清楚狀況，不斷發問阻礙了簡報進行時，可用下列這些句子。

☐ Please hold your questions until the end of my presentation.
請等我報告完畢後再發問。

☐ I'll be happy to deal with your questions after the conclusion of my presentation.
等我報告完畢，我會很樂意回答各位的問題。

☐ We really need to move on.
我們真的得繼續下去。

☐ Yes, what's your question, sir/ma'am?
是，先生／小姐，你的問題是？

☐ Maybe we can talk about this during the coffee break.
也許我們可以在點心時間討論這點。

☐ I'm not prepared to answer that question at this time.
我目前並沒有準備回答這個問題。

99 總結

用下列這些句子為報告收尾。

☐ To wrap up, I'd just like to say that the best solution to our biggest challenge is to take the steps I've just outlined.

最後我想說的是，如果要因應我們最大的挑戰，最好的辦法就是採取我剛才所提出的步驟。

☐ What we can conclude from all of this is that the economic downturn[1] is likely to continue for at least another quarter.

我們可以從這一切斷定說，經濟不景氣起碼可能會再持續一季。

☐ Just to recap,[2] let me repeat the main steps of the process.

為了簡述要點，我再把流程的主要步驟說一遍。

☐ Just to reiterate,[3] what I am saying is that the need to restructure the department is an urgent one.

再講一遍，我的意思是，部門有迫切的重建必要。

☐ To sum it all up, what we need is not additional sales channels, but more efficient manufacturing processes.

總歸一句話，我們需要的不是額外的銷售管道，而是更有效率的製造流程。

☐ I'd like to leave you with one thought: although change is difficult, complacency will spell[5] disaster for our firm.

我想給各位一個想法：改革雖然困難，但安於現狀卻會為公司帶來災難。

Word list

1 downturn [ˈdaʊntɝn] n. （經濟）衰退；下降

2 recap [riˈkæp] v. 【口語】重述重點

3 reiterate [riˈɪtəˌret] v. 重申；反覆講

4 complacency [kəmˈplesn̩sɪ] n. 滿足

5 spell [spɛl] v. 招致（後果）；變成……結果

100 接受及鼓勵提問

☐ I'd like to open the floor[1] for questions.
我想開放提問。

☐ Is there anyone that still has any doubts?
有人還有任何疑問嗎？

☐ Are there any questions?
有任何問題嗎？

☐ You, sir/ma'am, had a question earlier?
先生／小姐，你剛才有問題是嗎？

☐ Please, feel free to speak your mind.
請各位盡量說出你們的想法。

☐ Don't be afraid to speak up.
不要害怕提出意見。

Word list
1 floor [flor] *n.* （會議的）發言權

Part 14

協商合約

101 標準說法 1

☐ Everybody wants a win-win¹ situation here.

大家都希望在此創造雙贏的局面。

☐ You're not leaving me many options.

你沒有給我多少選擇。

☐ You're asking for a lot.

你的胃口很大。

☐ Try to see it from our point of view.

試著從我們的觀點來看。

☐ Can you up the offer?

你能把價錢出高一點嗎？

☐ All I'm asking for is a little flexibility.²

我要的不過就是一點彈性。

Word list

1 win-win [`wɪn`wɪn] *adj.* 雙贏的

2 flexibility [ˌflɛksə`bɪlətɪ] *n.* 彈性；通融性

102 標準說法 2

☐ I've been upfront[1] with you from the get-go.[2]

從一開始我就對你很坦白。

☐ We're willing to make concessions.[3]

我們願意讓步。

☐ How about a little quid pro quo?[4]

再互惠一點怎麼樣？

☐ What can you give me in return?

那你又可以給我什麼？

☐ I have absolutely no wiggle[5] room on this.

我在這方面絕對沒有一點商量的餘地。

☐ That's something I can't compromise[6] on.

我不會在這方面妥協。

Word list

[1] upfront [`ʌp͵frʌnt] *adj.* 直率的；坦白的

[2] get-go [`gɛt͵go] *n.* 【美口語】開始；開端

[3] concession [kən`sɛʃən] *n.* 讓步；讓步行為

[4] quid pro quo [͵kwɪd pro `kwo] *n.* 利益；交換；代替物；補償物

[5] wiggle [`wɪgl̩] *n.* 扭動；擺動

[6] compromise [`kɑmprə͵maɪz] *v.* 妥協

103 挽回買賣

在進展不順利時想挽回買賣，就可以說這些話。

☐ Why the sudden change of heart?
為什麼突然改變心意？

☐ I thought you were all gung-ho[1] about this.
我以為你們對這件事都很熱衷。

☐ I don't want to walk away from the table without a deal.
我不希望空手而回。

☐ I'd really hoped we could get something down on paper.
我真的希望我們能簽訂一些內容。

☐ I think we'll have to agree to disagree on that point.
我想我們必須在這點上求同存異。

☐ Let's not throw the baby out with the bathwater!
我們不要好壞不分、全盤否定！

Word list **1** gung-ho [`gʌŋ`ho] *adj.* 起勁的；熱心的

104 合作

☐ Let's put our heads together and see what we come up with.
我們來共商大計，看能提出什麼想法。

☐ It's imperative[1] for us to present a united front.
我們必須團結一致。

☐ We're willing to meet you halfway on this.[2]
我們願意在這點上做點讓步。

☐ I'm sure we can find some common ground here.
我相信我們能在這方面找到一些共同的基礎。

☐ It's in everyone's best interests to work together on this.
在這方面攜手合作對大家最有利。

☐ You scratch[3] my back; I'll scratch yours.
你幫我，我就幫你。

Part 14 協商合約

Word list
1 imperative [ɪmˋpɛrətɪv] *adj.* 非做不可的；必要的；緊要的
2 meet sb. halfway on sth. 在……遷就某人
3 scratch [skrætʃ] *v.* 搔（癢處等）

105 強勢出擊

☐ Let's get right to the point.

咱們就進入主題吧。

☐ Let's cut to the chase.

咱們廢話少說。

☐ The bottom line is this: We can't go a penny over ten million.

總歸一句話：我們就出一千萬，多加一分錢都不行。

☐ You should know you're up against[1] some stiff[2] competition.

你應該知道，你們面對了一些嚴厲的競爭對手。

☐ You're aware we have other offers on the table?

你知道我們在檯面上還有其他公司的出價吧？

☐ We're entertaining other offers.

我們還有其他人的報價。

Word list
1 up against 【口語】遭遇；面臨（困難、障礙等）
2 stiff [stɪf] *adj.* 困難的；辛苦的；難應付的

106 保密協定

CD2 44

☐ Everything said today will be held in strictest confidence.[1]
今天所說的一切要完全保密。

☐ Nothing said here today leaves this room.
今天在這裡所談的一切千萬不能洩漏出去。

☐ These are trade secrets and should be treated as such.
這些是商業機密,所以不該說的就不要說。

☐ None of this should be discussed with outside parties.
這些事禁止跟外人討論。

☐ These materials are/This information is for your eyes and ears only.
這些內容/訊息到你眼前為止。

☐ This meeting never happened — are we clear?
這次會議從來沒有發生過,明白嗎?

Word list　**1** in confidence 祕密地;私下地

107 詢問進展

重述並詢問目前的協商狀態。

☐ Where do we go from here?

我們下一步怎麼走？

☐ What's our next step?

我們的下一步是什麼？

☐ Where does that leave us?

我們現在該怎麼處理？

☐ So, what have we got so far?

所以到目前為止，我們有什麼進展？

☐ I think we've made some progress.

我想我們已經有了一些進展。

☐ I'm encouraged by what we've accomplished today.

我們今天的成果讓我深受鼓舞。

108 簽約

CD2 46

成交！把筆拿出來吧！

Part *14*

協

商

合

約

☐ You've got a deal!

生意是你的了！

☐ Let's ink[1] this deal!

我們來簽定這筆買賣吧！

☐ Let's put this baby to bed!

我們來把它敲定吧！

☐ It's a done deal!

成交！

☐ Ladies and gentlemen, you've got yourselves a deal.

各位，你們已經拿到了這筆生意！

☐ Looks like we've got ourselves a deal.

看來我們拿到這筆生意了！

Word list　**1** ink [ɪŋk] *v.*【美俚語】簽署；簽訂（合約）

Part **15**

交　際

109 建議用餐

☐ That's enough for today. Let's get something to eat.

今天到此為止。我們去吃點東西吧。

☐ I'm starving.[1] How about you?

我餓了。你呢？

☐ What do you say we get a bite to eat?

我們去吃點東西，你覺得怎麼樣？

☐ I'm famished.[2] Do you know any good restaurants nearby?

我好餓。你知道附近有什麼好餐廳嗎？

☐ What's the plan for lunch/dinner?

午餐／晚餐打算吃什麼？

☐ Let's break for lunch.

我們去休息吃午飯吧。

Word list
1 starving [`stɑrvɪŋ] adj. 挨餓的；飢餓的
2 famished [`fæmɪʃt] adj. 非常飢餓的

110 建議喝一杯

☐ I'm ready for a drink. How about you?

我準備要去喝一杯。你呢？

☐ I'm parched.¹ How about a drink?

我渴斃了。去喝一杯怎麼樣？

☐ Do you feel like getting a drink somewhere?

你想不想找個地方喝一杯？

☐ I need to unwind.² Let's get a drink.

我得放鬆一下。我們去喝一杯吧。

☐ We can still catch happy hour!

我們還是可以去開心一下！

☐ Care for a drink/nightcap?³

想去喝點東西／一杯睡前酒嗎？

Word
list

1 parched [pɑrtʃd] *adj.* 【口語】喉嚨乾渴的

2 unwind [ʌnˋwaɪnd] *v.* 【口語】使（人）心情放鬆

3 nightcap [ˋnaɪtˌkæp] *n.* 【口語】*n.* 夜酒；睡前酒

111 建議活動

☐ Anybody up for some karaoke?

有沒有人要去唱卡拉 OK ？

☐ I'd love to get in a round of golf/game of squash.[1]

我想去打場高爾夫球／回力球。

☐ There's a movie I'd like to see. I wonder if it's showing[2] anywhere around here.

我想去看一部電影。不曉得這附近有沒有哪裡在播。

☐ I'd like to take in[3] some of the local culture.

我想去體驗一下本地的文化。

☐ What do you do for fun around here?

這附近有什麼好玩的？

☐ You mentioned it might be possible to see a musical[4]/an
opera/a play while I'm here.

你之前說過，我在這裡的時候也許看得到歌舞劇／歌劇／話劇。

Word
list
1 squash [skwɑʃ] *n.* 回力球 （一種兩人或四人對打的室內球戲）

2 show [ʃo] *n.* 上演（電影、戲劇等）

3 take in 【美口語】出席；遊覽；參觀

4 musical [ˋmjuzɪk!] *n.* 音樂劇

112　接受／婉拒邀約

第一句是用於你晚上有精神去玩的時候。其他的則適用於你只想休息的時候。

精神好時

☐ I'm up for¹ anything.
　我玩什麼都行。

疲憊不堪時

☐ I'm not up for anything too wild.
　我不想玩得太瘋。

☐ I can't have a late night.
　我沒辦法熬夜。

☐ Let's call it a night.²
　我們今晚就到此為止吧。

☐ We've got an early start tomorrow.
　我們明天一早就要辦事了。

☐ I'm beat.³ I'm going to hit the sack.⁴
　我不行了。我要去躺平了。

Word list
1 up for　打算
2 call it a night　【口語】結束今夜的工作；今夜到此結束
3 beat [bit] *adj.* 疲乏的（不用在名詞前）
4 sack [sæk] *n.* 【美俚】床；睡袋

113 | 點酒

☐ I'll have a scotch[1] on the rocks.[2]
　我要威士忌加冰。

☐ What do you have on tap?
　你們有哪些生啤酒？

☐ Do you have any imports?[3]
　你們有進口的生啤酒嗎？

☐ Can I take a look at the wine list?
　我能不能看看酒單？

☐ Let's get a pitcher[4] of Stella Artois.
　我們來一桶 Stella Artois 好了。

☐ A bottle of your finest champagne![5]
　來一瓶你們最好的香檳！

Word list

1 scotch [skɑtʃ] n. 【口語】蘇格蘭威士忌
2 on the rocks （飲料）加冰塊
3 import [`ɪmport] n. 進口貨

4 pitcher [`pɪtʃɚ] n. 水罐；水瓶
5 champagne [ʃæm`pen] n. 香檳酒

114 點餐

☐ I'm going to have the Filet Mignon.[1]
我要吃菲力牛排。

☐ I'm going to go with the braised[2] lamb.
我要點燉羊肉。

☐ The mixed platter sounds good to me.
拼盤聽起來不錯。

☐ I've been craving[3] some fresh seafood/a steak.
我一直想來一點海鮮／一客牛排。

☐ That looks good. What are they having?
那看起來不錯。他們吃的是什麼？

☐ I'll have the same.
我要一樣的。

Word
list
1 Filet Mignon [fɪ`le `mɪnjɑn] *n.* 非列牛排
2 braised [brezd] *a.* 燉煮的；蒸的
3 crave [krev] *v.* 渴望；熱望

115

要求服務

頭兩句是對餐桌上的其他人說，其他的則是說給服務生聽。

☐ Could you please pass the salt?

可不可以麻煩你把鹽遞給我？

☐ I'll have a little more rice, thanks.

我還要一點飯，謝謝。

☐ Could I have a new knife/fork[1]/spoon, please?

可以麻煩給我一支新的刀子／叉子／湯匙嗎？

☐ Could you bring us some condiments[2] please?

可以麻煩你給我一些調味料嗎？

☐ We need one more place setting.[3]

我們還需要一份餐具。

☐ It's rather cold/hot. Do you think you could turn up/turn down the air conditioning?

有點冷／熱。你們可以把空調開大／小一點嗎？

Word list
1 fork [fɔrk] *n.* 叉子
2 condiment [ˋkɑndəmənt] *n.* 佐料；調味料
3 place setting [ˋples ˏsɛtɪŋ] *n.* （餐桌上個人使用的）餐位餐具

116 敬酒

舉杯時可以說這些話。

☐ I'd like to propose a toast[1] — to our continued cooperation and mutual[2] profits.

我想為我們的繼續合作與互利乾一杯。

☐ A toast: to our new joint venture![3]

為我們新的合資企業乾一杯！

☐ Ladies and gentlemen, raise your glasses with me.

各位，請跟我一起舉杯。

☐ Let's celebrate another ten years of partnership!

我們來慶祝另一個合作的十年！

☐ Let's drink to our continued success.

為我們持續的成功喝一杯。

☐ To your health!

祝各位身體健康！

Word list

1 propose a toast 提議為⋯⋯乾杯（toast [`tost] *n.* 乾杯；舉杯祝賀）

2 mutual [`mjutʃuəl] *adj.* 互相的；共同的；共通的

3 joint venture [`dʒɔɪnt `vɛntʃɚ] *n.* 合資企業

117 訂位／更改訂位

☐ How many in your party?

你們有多少人？

☐ Would you like smoking or non-smoking?

你們要吸菸區還是非吸菸區？

☐ No problem.

沒問題。

☐ I'm sorry. We're booked solid.[1]

抱歉，我們訂滿了。

☐ We have nothing/no tables available at that time.

我們那個時間沒有空位。

☐ How about 12:30? That's the best I can do.

十二點半怎麼樣？我只能做到這樣了。

Word list **1** solid [`salɪd] *adj.* 完全的

118 訂位／更改訂位

CD2 56

你可能要負責帶客戶去外面用餐。當你打電話給餐廳時，可以說這些話。

☐ I'd like to reserve a table for eight at six-thirty.
我想訂位，八個人，六點半。

☐ Do you have a table in non-smoking?
你們的非吸菸區有位子嗎？

☐ Do you have private dining rooms/private booths?
你們有貴賓廳／包廂嗎？

☐ Three members of our party are vegetarians.[1]
我們宴會有三個人吃素。

☐ Can I change my reservation to seven o'clock?
我能把訂位改成七點嗎？

☐ I'll take it!
那就這樣！

Part
15
交
際

Word list **1** vegetarian [ˌvɛdʒəˈtɛrɪən] *n.* 素食（主義）者／ *adj.* 素食（主義）者的

119 談公事

可用這些句子回顧當天的經過或討論新的生意。

☐ I thought today went well.

我覺得今天進行得很順利。

☐ I'm glad we covered so much ground.[1]

很高興我們討論了這麼多。

☐ Things went as well as we could have expected.

事情就跟我們所預期的一樣順利。

☐ We did a good thing today, ladies and gentlemen.

各位,我們今天表現得不錯。

☐ There's something else I'd like to discuss that I didn't bring up earlier.

我想討論我前面沒有提到的另外一件事。

☐ I still have some concerns about the third-party coverage[2] issue.

我還是有點擔心第三責任險的問題。

Word list **1** cover (the) ground 前進(某段距離);(演說者等)涉及某範圍
2 coverage [`kʌvərɪdʒ] n. 涵蓋範圍;保險項目(範圍)

120 避談公事

有時候夠了就是夠了。這些話應該帶著笑容開玩笑地說，而不要太嚴肅。

☐ No shop talk![1]

別再談公事了！

☐ Let's leave the office in the office.

我們把公事留在公司吧。

☐ Let's not mix business with pleasure. We're here to drink/dance/enjoy the show!

我們不要在玩樂的時候談生意。到這裡來就是要喝酒／跳舞／看表演！

☐ Stop worrying about it! You need to unwind.

別再擔心了！你需要放鬆。

☐ I'll talk about anything but work.

除了工作以外，我什麼都聊。

☐ All work and no play makes me an unhappy girl. Let's mambo![2]

只工作不玩樂會讓我變悶。我們來跳曼波吧！

Word list

1 shop talk [`ʃɑp ˌtɔlk] *n.* 談論公事

2 mambo [`mɑmbo] *v.* 跳曼波

121 請客

在餐廳裡

☐ It's my treat, I insist.

我請客,沒得商量。

☐ Dinner's on me. Or should I say, on the company!

晚餐我請。或者我應該說,由公司請才對!

☐ I've already taken care of it.

我已經買單了。

在酒吧裡

☐ This round's on me.

這輪算我的。

☐ I've got this/the next round.

這輪/下輪我請客。

☐ I'll put it on my tab.[1]

我來買單。

Word list **1** tab [tæb] *n.*【美口語】*n.* 帳單 (= bill)

122 搶著付帳

當你們為了搶付帳而爭執不下時，就可以說這些話。

☐ Let me get it!

讓我來！

☐ Please, I insist.

拜託，一定要讓我來。

☐ The expense account takes care of these things!

這些東西可以報帳！

☐ That's what an expense account is for, isn't it?

交際費就是用來做這個的，不是嗎？

☐ Your money's no good here!

這裡輪不到你付錢！

☐ The boss would kill me if he/she knew I let you pay!

假如老闆知道我讓你出錢，他／她會殺了我！

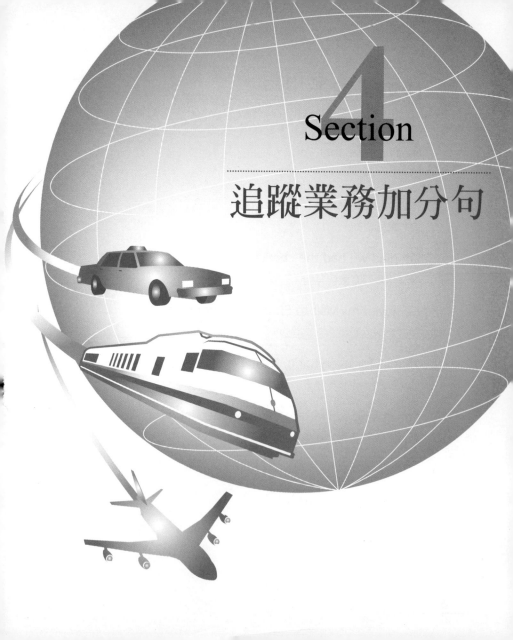

Section
4

追蹤業務加分句

☐ Nice to have met you.

很開心認識你。

☐ It was a pleasure to meet you.

很高興認識你。

☐ I'm glad we had the chance to meet.

很高興我們有機會見面。

☐ I enjoyed my visit to Shanghai very much.

我這次來上海參訪非常開心。

☐ Thanks for everything. I can't wait for my next trip here.

感激不盡。我等不及下次再來這裡了。

☐ I'm looking forward to our next meeting/visit.

期待下次再見面／拜訪。

124 寄送資料

CD2 62

出差回來之後，務必記得請內勤人員幫你寄出出差時允諾顧客要給他們的資料。

☐ I'm sending out the information/samples you requested.
我正要把你要的資料／樣本寄給你。

☐ The information I'm sending should answer all your questions.
我所寄的資料應該能回答你所有的問題。

☐ The information/samples went out this morning/yesterday.
資料／樣本今天早上／昨天就寄出來了。

☐ I'll get that information/those samples out to you right away.
我會立刻把這些資料／樣本寄給你。

☐ You wanted some information/samples. I'm on it!
你要的一些資料／樣本，我正在處理！

☐ I'm surprised you didn't get it. I'll try sending it out again.
我很意外你沒有收到。我會試著再寄一次。

125 繼續／終止生意往來

CD2 63

可用這些話代為宣布老闆的決定。

☐ I'm happy to announce the boss has said we'll be doing business with you.

我要很高興地宣布，老闆說我們要跟你們做生意。

☐ I'm/the boss is impressed.[1] You're in!

我／老闆覺得很不錯。你們中選了！

☐ After what we've seen, you are our first choice!

在我們看過以後，你們是我們的第一選擇！

☐ The boss had a change of heart.[2] Looks like we will be doing business after all.

老闆改變了心意。看來我們肯定會做生意了。

☐ Sorry, the boss pulled the plug on that idea.[3]

抱歉，老闆回絕了那個想法。

☐ Sorry, the boss has decided to go with someone else.

抱歉，老闆決定選別人。

Word list
[1] impressed [ɪmˋpɛst] *adj.* 深受感動的；銘記……的
[2] have a change of heart 改變心意
[3] pull the plug on sth. 終止；廢除

126 繼續推銷

CD2 64

這些話可在電話或電子郵件中使用。

☐ You mentioned in passing you might be interested in expanding.[1]

你稍有提到，你們可能對擴廠有興趣。

☐ You expressed a lot of interest in opening a franchise[2] here.

你們說過很有興趣在這裡設新廠。

☐ We had talked about you doing some marketing for us, too.

我們也談過請你們來幫我們做一點行銷。

☐ I've looked into it, and we'll be able to do the job for you/ deliver by the end of the month.

我研究過了，我們可以幫你們做這件事／月底就以送出。

☐ We'd agreed that you'd handle all local sales.

我們同意由你們來負責當地所有的銷售。

☐ Did you get a chance to think about what I said to you at the trade show?

你有機會考慮一下我在商展上對你說的話嗎？

Word list

1 expand [ɪks`pænd] *v.* 擴大；擴張

2 franchise [`fræntʃaɪz] *n.* （經銷商所授與某特定地區的）經銷權

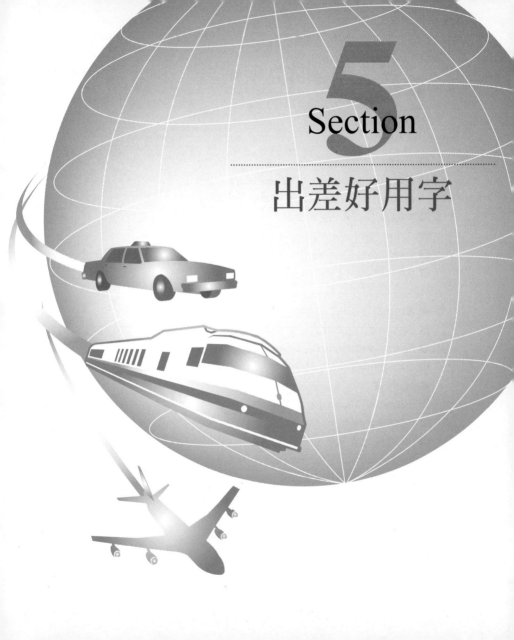

Section

5

出差好用字

127 旅客常見疾病

小毛病

1 head cold [`hɛd ˌkold] *n.* 感冒

2 nasal congestion [`nezl`kɛndʒɛstʃən] *n.* 鼻塞／
runny nose [`rʌnɪ `noz] *n.* 流鼻涕

3 sneeze [`sniz] *v./n.* 打噴嚏

4 cough [kɔf] *v./n.* 咳嗽

5 sore throat [`sor `θrot] *n.* 喉嚨痛

6 stomachache [`stʌməkˌek] *n.* 胃痛；腹痛

其他症狀

7 allergy [`ælədʒɪ] *n.* 過敏

8 diabetes [ˌdaɪə`bitiz] *n.* 糖尿病 / diabetic [ˌdaɪə`bɛtɪk] *n.* 糖尿病患者

9 heart palpitations [`hɑrt ˌpælpɪ`teʃənz] *n.* 心悸

10 arrhythmia [ə`rɪθmɪə] *n.* 心律不整

11 heart attack [`hɑrt ə`tæk] *n.* 心臟病

12 dizziness [`dɪzənɪs] *n.* 暈眩

13 nausea [`nɔʃɪə] *n.* 噁心

14 pain [pen] *n.* 疼痛

15 food poisoning [`fud ˌpɔɪznɪŋ] *n.* 食物中毒

16 infection [ɪn`fɛkʃən] *n.* 感染

可避免的疾病

17 sunstroke [`sʌnˌstrok] *n.* 中暑

18 heat exhaustion [`hit ɪg`zɔstʃən] *n.* 熱衰竭

19 dehydration [ˌdihaɪ`dreʃən] *n.* 脫水

20 sunburn [`sʌnˌbɝn] *v./n.* 曬傷

128 成藥

症狀	藥名
cold [kold] *n.* 感冒	Vicks Dayquil [`vɪks `dekwɪl] *n.* 維克戴奎爾綜合感冒藥（日用） Vicks Nyquil [`vɪks `naɪkwɪl] *n.* 維克奈奎爾綜合感冒藥（夜用）
constipation [ˌkɑnstə`peʃən] *n.* 便秘	Correctol [kə`rɛktəl] *n.* 可瑞妥瀉劑
cough [kɔf] *n.* 咳嗽	Cepacol [`sɪpəkɔl] *n.* 瑟培可糖錠
diarrhea [ˌdaɪə`riə] *n.* 腹瀉	Imodium AD [ɪ`modɪəm `e `di] *n.* 痢達膠囊
headache [`hɛdˌek] *n.* 頭痛	Aleve [`æliv] *n.* 艾力弗藥丸 Excedrin [ɪk`sɛdrɪn] *n.* 伊克賽錠
insect bite [`ɪnsɛkt ˌbaɪt] *n.* 蚊蟲咬傷	After Bite [`æftə ˌbaɪt] *n.* 蚊蟲叮咬擦劑
muscle ache [`mʌsḷ ˌek] *n.* 肌肉痠痛	Bengay [bɛn`ge] *n.* 奔肌乳膏
rash [ræʃ] *n.* 長疹子	A+D Ointment [`ɔɪntmənt] *n.* A 加 D 軟膏
stomach ache [`stʌmək ˌek] *n.* 胃痛	Pepto-Bismol [`pɛptə`bɪzmɔl] *n.* 百託必司模胃藥
sunburn [`sʌnˌbɚn] *n.* 曬傷	Solarcaine [`solɚˌken] *n.* 速樂康噴霧

129 飯店設施及服務

客房種類

1 deluxe room [dɪ`lʌks `rum] *n.* 豪華客房

2 superior room [sə`pɪrɪɚ `rum] *n.* 精緻客房

3 executive room [ɪg`zɛkjʊtɪv `rum] *n.* 行政客房

4 presidential suite [`prɛzədɛnʃəl `swit] *n.* 總統套房

設施及用品

5 iron [`aɪɚn] *n.* 熨斗

6 ironing board [`aɪɚnɪŋ ˌbord] *n.* 燙衣板

7 bathtub [`bæθˌtʌb] *n.* 浴缸

8 hair dryer [`hɛr `draɪɚ] *n.* 吹風機

9 sewing kit [`soɪŋ `kɪt] *n.* 針線包

10 satellite television [`sætḷˌaɪt `tɛləˌvɪʒən] *n.* 衛星電視／
cable [`kebḷ] *n.* 有線電視

11 safety deposit box [`seftɪ dɪ`pɑzɪt ˌbɑks] *n.* 保險箱

12 air conditioning [`ɛr kən`dɪʃənɪŋ] *n.* 空調系統

13 wireless Internet access [`waɪrlɪs `ɪntɚnɛt `æksɛs] *n.* 無線上網

服務

14 florist [`florɪst] *n.* 花店；花商

15 laundromat [`lɑndrəmæt] *n.* 自助洗衣店

16 luggage storage [`lʌgɪʤ `storɪʤ] *n.* 行李寄放

17 collect call [kə`lɛkt ˌkɔl] *n.* 對方付費電話

18 valet parking [`vælɪt ˌpɑrkɪŋ] *n.* 代客泊車

19 spa [spɑ] *n.* 水療

20 gym [ʤɪm] *n.* 健身房／weight room [`wet ˌrum] 重量訓練室

130 餐廳類型

餐廳類型

1 bar and grill [`bɑr ˏɛnd ˏgrɪl] *n.* 烤肉餐館

2 bistro [`bistro] *n.* 小型酒館；小飯館

3 buffet [bə`fe] *n.* 自助式餐廳

4 café [kə`fe] *n.* 咖啡店；露天餐館

5 coffee shop [`kɔfɪ `ʃɑp] / coffeehouse [`kɔfɪˏhaʊs] *n.* 咖啡館

6 diner [`daɪnɚ] / greasy spoon [`grisɪ ˏspun] *n.* 簡餐店

7 dive [daɪv] *n.* 廉價餐廳

8 family restaurant [`fæmlɪ `rɛstərənt] *n.* 家庭餐廳

9 hole in the wall [`hol ˏɪn ˏðə `wɔl] *n.* 小店

10 pub [pʌb] / tavern [`tævɚn] *n.* 酒吧；酒館

以料理區分的餐廳種類

11 burger joint [`bɝgɚ `dʒɔɪnt] *n.* 漢堡連鎖店

12 deli=delicatessen [ˏdɛləkə`tɛsn̩] *n.* 熟食店；現成食品店（大部分以賣三明治為主）

13 oyster bar [`ɔɪstɚ `bɑr] *n.* 蠔肉吧

14 pancake house [`pænˏkek ˏhaʊs] *n.* 煎餅屋 ／
waffle house [`wɑfl̩ ˏhaʊs] *n.* 鬆餅屋

15 pizzeria [ˏpitsə`riə] *n.* 披薩餅店

16 ribs joint [`ribs ˏdʒɔɪnt] *n.* 肋排連鎖店

17 steak house [`stek ˏhaʊs] *n.* 牛排館

18 taqueria [ˏtɑkə`riɑ] *n.* 墨式餐廳

19 trattoria [ˏtrɑtə`riɑ] *n.* 廉價義式餐館

20 vegetarian restaurant [ˏvɛdʒə`tɛrɪən `rɛstərənt] *n.* 素食餐廳

131 展館用語

1. booth [buθ] *n.* 攤位
2. counter [`kauntɚ] *n.* 櫃台
3. signage [`saɪnɪʤ] *n.* 招牌／sign [saɪn] *n.* 看板
4. lighting [`laɪtɪŋ] *n.* 燈明
5. logo [`logo] *n.* 商標／mark [mɑrk] *n.* 標誌
6. display [dɪ`sple] *n.* 展示
7. demo [`dɛmo] *n.* 宣傳帶
8. demonstration model [͵dɛmən`streʃən `mɑdl̩] *n.* 展示模型
9. sample [`sæmpl̩] *n.* 樣品
10. promo material [`promo ͵mə`tɪrɪəl] *n.* 促銷資料
11. brochure [bro`ʃur] *n.* 簡介
12. pamphlet [`pæmflɪt] *n.* 小冊子
13. business card [`bɪznɪs `kɑrd] *n.* 名片
14. giveaway [`gɪvə͵we] *n.* 贈品
15. crowd [kraud] *n.* 人群
16. model [`mɑdl̩] *n.* 模型
17. rep [rɛp] (= representative [rɛprɪ`zɛntətɪv]) 代表
18. salesman [`selzmən] / saleswoman [`selz͵wumən] *n.* 推銷員
19. spokesman [`spoksmən] / spokeswoman [`spoks͵wumən] *n.* 發言人
20. delegate [`dɛləgɪt] *n.* 代表人

132 簡報視聽設備

電腦暨周邊設備

1. hard drive [`hɑrd `draɪv] *n.* 硬碟
2. software [`sɔft,wɛr] *n.* 軟體
3. high-resolution monitor [`haɪ,rɛzə`luʃən mɑnətɚ] *n.* 高解析顯示器
4. port [port] *n.* 埠
5. interface [`ɪntɚ,fes] *n.* 介面
6. compatible [kəm`pætəbl] *adj.* 相容
7. storage [`storɪdʒ] *n.* 儲存體
8. keyboard [`ki,bord] *n.* 鍵盤
9. electrical cord [ɪ`lɛktrɪkl `kord] *n.* 電線／cable [`kebl] *n.* 電纜線
10. outlet [`aut,lɛt] *n.* 插座
11. battery [`bætərɪ] *n.* 電池
12. charger [`tʃɑrdʒɚ] *n.* 充電器

其他硬體

13. slide [slaɪd] *n.* 幻燈片
14. projector [prə`dʒɛktɚ] *n.* 投影機
15. screen [skrin] *n.* 屏；幕
16. laser pointer [`lezɚ ,pɔɪntɚ] *n.* 雷射光筆
17. public address system [`pʌblɪk ə`drɛs ,sɪstəm] *n.* 擴音裝置 (= PA system)
18. microphone [`maɪkrə,fon] *n.* 麥克風
19. flat-screen TV [`flæt,skrin `ti`vi] *n.* 平面電視
20. volume [`vɑljəm] *n.* 音量

133 　數字和單位　　　　　　　　　　　　　　　　

1　1/4 = a/one-fourth/quarter（四分之一）

2　1/3 = a/one-third（三分之一）

3　1/2 = a/one-half（二分之一）

4　2/3 = two-thirds（三分之二）

5　3/4 = three-fourths/quarters（四分之三）

6　22/7 = twenty-two sevenths（七分之二十二）

7　3.14 = three point one four（三點一四）

8　66.6% = sixty-six point six percent（百分之六十六點六）

9　25% off = twenty-five percent off（七五折）

10　1×10^2 = one times ten squared（一乘十的二次方）

11　2×10^{-3} = two times ten to the negative third
　　（二乘十的負三次方）

12　5 ft^2 = five square feet（五平方英呎）

13　9 ft^3 = nine cubic feet（九立方英呎）

14　7 psi = seven pounds per square inch（每平方英吋七磅）

15　35 mph = thirty-five miles per hour（每小時三十五哩）

16　75°F = seventy-five degrees (Fahrenheit)（華氏七十五度）

17　-10°F = ten below zero (Fahrenheit)（華氏零下十度）

18　-15°C = minus fifteen degrees (Celsius)（攝氏零下十五度）

134　錢的相關說法

☐ Fifty bucks[1]/smackers[2]/quid![3] That's ridiculous!

50 美元 / 美元 / 英磅！太誇張了！

☐ Twenty grand[4] is a lot of moola[5]/cash/dough![6]

2 萬美金是很大一筆錢 / 現金 / 現款！

☐ Can you break this bill for me, please?

請將這張紙鈔換開好嗎？

☐ I'd like two twenties and a ten for this fifty.

這張 50 美元紙鈔，我想換成 2 張 20 元紙鈔和 1 張 10 元紙鈔。

☐ I need change for a dollar. Two quarters, four dimes[7], a nickel[8] and five pennies, please.

我要把 1 美元換開。請給我 2 枚 25 分幣、4 枚 10 分幣、1 枚 5 分幣和 5 枚 1 分幣。

☐ I've got my mind on my money and my money on my mind.

我老掛記著錢，錢也始終在我心上。

Word list

1 buck [bʌk] *n.* 一美元

2 smacker [`smækɚ] *n.*【俚】美元

3 quid [kwɪd] *n.*【俚】一英鎊

4 grand [grænd] *n.*【俚】千元

5 moola [`mulə] *n.*【俚】金錢

6 dough [do] *n.* 錢；現金

7 dime [daɪm] *n.* 一角硬幣

8 nickel [`nɪkl] *n.* 五分鎳幣

附錄 1

國　際　小　費　標　準		
Australia（澳洲）		10-15%
Austria（奧地利）		5-10%
Belgium（比利時）		無
Britain（英國）		10-15%
Canada（加拿大）		15-20%
Denmark（丹麥）		帳單已內含
Finland（芬蘭）		帳單已內含
France（法國）		帳單已內含（加給零錢）
Germany（德國）		帳單已內含（加給零錢）
Greece（希臘）		帳單已內含（加給零錢）
Hong Kong（香港）		10%
Ireland（愛爾蘭）		10%
Italy（義大利）		帳單已內含（加給零錢）
Japan（日本）		無
Mexico（墨西哥）		15%
Netherlands（荷蘭）		帳單已內含（加給零錢）
New Zealand（紐西蘭）		5-10%
Norway（挪威）		帳單已內含
Portugal（葡萄牙）		10%
Singapore（新加坡）		無
South Korea（南韓）		無
Spain（西班牙）		帳單已內含（加給零錢）
Sweden（瑞典）		帳單已內含
Switzerland（瑞士）		帳單已內含（加給零錢）
Thailand（泰國）		無
United States（美國）		15-20%

資料來源：經 Tramex Travel 授權同意使用
http://www.tramex.com/tips/tipping.htm

附錄 2

各 國 免 稅 商 品 額 度 比 較

台　　　　　灣

200 支香菸（或 25 支雪茄；或 1 磅菸葉）。

1 瓶不超過 1,000 毫升的餐酒 (wine) 或烈酒 (spirit)。

價值不超過 20,000 新台幣的物品。

泰　　　　　國

200 支香菸（或 250 公克雪茄；或 250 公克菸葉）。

1 公升餐酒或烈酒。

價值一千泰銖之個人物品。

法　　　　　國

200 支香菸（或 100 支小雪茄；或 50 支雪茄；或
250 公克菸葉）。

1 公升烈酒（或 2 公升餐酒）。

50 公克香精和 250 毫升香水。

美　　　　　國

200 支香菸（或 50 支雪茄；或 2 公斤菸絲）。

1 公升餐酒（二十一歲以上旅客）。

非美國居民可免稅攜帶不超過 100 美元的物品。

美國居民可免稅攜帶相等於 800 美元的物品。

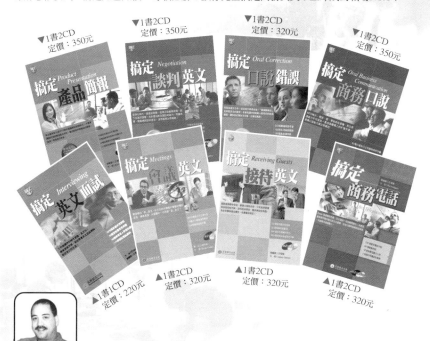

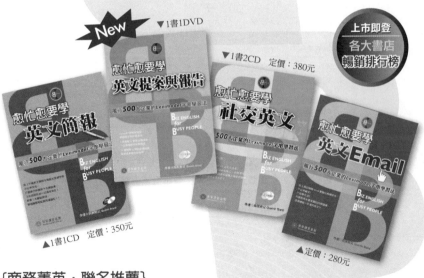

國家圖書館出版品預行編目資料

出差 900 句典 / Jason Grenier 作；戴至中譯.
——初版.——臺北市：貝塔，2006〔民 95〕
　　面：　　公分

　ISBN 957-729-570-3（平裝附光碟片）

　1. 商業英語—會話

805.188　　　　　　　　　　　　94026418

出差 900 句典

Overheard on a Business Trip

作　　　者 / Jason Grenier
審　　　訂 / 梁欣榮
譯　　　者 / 戴至中
執 行 編 輯 / 莊碧娟

出　　　版 / 貝塔出版有限公司
地　　　址 / 台北市 100 館前路 12 號 11 樓
電　　　話 / (02)2314-2525
傳　　　真 / (02)2312-3535
郵　　　撥 / 19493777 貝塔出版有限公司
客服專線 / (02)2314-3535
客服信箱 / btservice@betamedia.com.tw

總 經 銷 / 時報文化出版企業股份有限公司
地　　　址 / 桃園縣龜山鄉萬壽路二段 351 號
電　　　話 / (02) 2306-6842

出版日期 / 2006 年 2 月初版一刷
定　　　價 / 250 元
ISBN： 957-729-570-3

喚醒你的英文語感！

請對折後釘好，直接寄回即可！

廣　告　回　信
北區郵政管理局登記證
北 台 字 第 1 4 2 5 6 號
免　貼　郵　票

100 台北市中正區館前路12號11樓

 貝塔語言出版 收
Beta Multimedia Publishing

 □□□

貝塔語言出版
Beta Multimedia Publishing

讀者服務專線（02）2314-3535　　讀者服務傳真（02）2312-3535
客戶服務信箱 btservice@betamedia.com.tw

www.betamedia.com.tw

謝謝您購買本書！！

貝塔語言擁有最優良之英文學習書籍，為提供您最佳的英語學習資訊，您可填妥此表後寄回（免貼郵票）將可不定期收到本公司最新發行書訊及活動訊息！

姓名：_____　性別：□男 □女　生日：____年____月____日

電話：(公)_____(宅)_____(手機)_____

電子信箱：_____

學歷：□高中職含以下 □專科 □大學 □研究所含以上

職業：□金融 □服務 □傳播 □製造 □資訊 □軍公教 □出版

　　　□自由 □教育 □學生 □其他

職級：□企業負責人 □高階主管 □中階主管 □職員 □專業人士

1. 您購買的書籍是？_____

2. 您從何處得知本產品？(可複選)

　　　□書店 □網路 □書展 □校園活動 □廣告信函 □他人推薦 □新聞報導 □其他

3. 您覺得本產品價格：

　　　□偏高 □合理 □偏低

4. 請問目前您每週花了多少時間學英語？

　　　□ 不到十分鐘 □ 十分鐘以上，但不到半小時 □ 半小時以上，但不到一小時

　　　□ 一小時以上，但不到兩小時 □ 兩個小時以上 □ 不一定

5. 通常在選擇語言學習書時，哪些因素是您會考慮的？

　　　□ 封面 □ 內容、實用性 □ 品牌 □ 媒體、朋友推薦 □ 價格□ 其他_____

6. 市面上您最需要的語言書種類為？

　　　□ 聽力 □ 閱讀 □ 文法 □口說 □ 寫作 □ 其他_____

7. 通常您會透過何種方式選購語言學習書籍？

　　　□ 書店門市 □ 網路書店 □ 郵購 □ 直接找出版社 □ 學校或公司團購

　　　□ 其他_____

8. 給我們的建議：_____

_____

喚醒你的英文語感 ！

Get a Feel for English !

喚醒你的英文語感！

Get a Feel for English !

Get a Feel for English !

 喚醒你的英文語感!